Christmas Stalkings

Ten Tales of Literary Spirits

Todd Pettigrew
Scott Sharplin
Ken Chisholm
Jenn Tubrett

Editors
Sherry D. Ramsey I Julie A. Serroul I Nancy SM Waldman

Third Person Press

Third Person Press
Email: thirdpersonpress@gmail.com
Web: thirdpersonpress.com
Cape Breton, Nova Scotia, Canada
Published in Canada

Christmas Stalkings
Print Version ISBN: 978-0-9936325-2-5
Electronic Version ISBN: 978-0-9936325-3-2

Also from
Third Person Press

THE SPECULATIVE ELEMENTS SERIES

Undercurrents
Airborne
Unearthed
Flashpoint

OTHER TITLES

To Unimagined Shores,
Collected Stories by Sherry D. Ramsey

Grey Area, 13 Ghost Stories

Third
Person
Press

Contents

Introduction

In the fall of 2010 I was approached by staff at the McConnell Library in Sydney, Nova Scotia to see if members of my department at Cape Breton University might be interested in speaking to their seniors' book group about any of the various authors they intended to study. I myself was not expert in any of the writers they mentioned, but it did occur to me that the group might appreciate the works of one of my favourite novelists, Robertson Davies — an author I could speak about with some confidence. Alas, it turned out that funds were limited and there was no chance of buying new copies of Davies' novels.

Hearing this, it occurred to me if money was tight, what was needed was a fund raiser. Since the fifteenth anniversary of Davies' death and Christmas itself were both approaching, it occurred to me that a reading of Davies' Christmas ghost stories, collected in his book *High Spirits*, might be just the thing. The library agreed, and so it was. Every year since, the library has hosted an enchanted evening of spectres and spectacle, and hundreds of dollars have been raised to support the seniors' book group.

But even as the annual event had success, it became apparent we were going to run out of Davies' stories and that, in any case, it might be fun to create stories of our own. And so gradually, the Davies stories were replaced by original tales.

A selection of those tales is included here. We hope you find them as amusing as the original audiences did.

Todd Pettigrew
Cape Breton University
2016

Todd Pettigrew

A Chat with the Master

It was my firm intention to read to you tonight one of the delightful stories from Robertson Davies, as has been our tradition here at the library the past few years. But last week I had an experience that forced me to reconsider.

Now, those who know me know that I am not a superstitious man. In fact, even my friends might put me a little *too* far to the side of reason if it came to that. *Cold* is a word that has even been applied to my mental faculties — rather uncharitably in my opinion. But I digress.

I mean only to suggest that until last week I had regarded the stories we have been reading as the merest fancy. A winter's tale for a long night, as the Bard would have said. *Humbug*, to use a term appropriate to the season. And any attempt to cast a pall of truth over them was merely a rhetorical flourish to enhance the thrilling effect of the fiction.

Or so I thought.

It happened a week ago Tuesday, as I sat alone in my study — my then wife, as she frequently was, occupied elsewhere with her roller derby league. I was looking over my chosen story for the evening, a wonderful yarn called "The Spirit who Wouldn't Circulate," set in the Massey College Library — a chilling narrative even by the standards of Robertson Davies — when I heard a noise downstairs.

Now my house is populated, if not to say infested, with cats, so strange sounds on a dark night are nothing out of the ordinary. In fact, I normally become nervous only when the bumps in the night cease. In that case, I worry that my feline companions are planning a household mutiny.

But this sound was not of the cat variety.

This was the sound, strangely loud, of turning pages. And while I have known the cats to chew the corners of books and even to fold down the corners of pages, they have never been great or methodical readers.

Rising from my work, then, I cautiously took a few steps down the hall and stood at the top of the stairs. There it was again! A distinct—eerily distinct—sound of rustling paper coming from...the dining room?

Yes, I thought, *the dining room.*

I should here point out that the room that my wife and I call the dining room is so crammed with two lifetimes' worth of books, that it is not so much a dining room as a small, badly-organized library with a dining table in the middle.

After a long moment's deliberation, I decided that it was unlikely a potential murderer or even burglar would pause in the dining room to catch up on *The Hunger Games* (my wife's, of course). And so I bravely headed down the stairs, thinking perhaps a university colleague, Dr. Christie, our drama specialist, had taken the liberty of consulting my copy of a *Dictionary of Stage Directions in Renaissance Plays.*

But as I reached the foot of the stair, I knew that this was no professor visiting. Or, at least, no ordinary professor. For the whole of the lower floor of the house was bathed in a warm, yet strangely cool, golden glow.

As I passed through the living room adjacent to the source of the mysterious light, my heart skipped a beat. Or, possibly two. Who has the presence of mind to count at such a time? For there, in my very own dining room library, sat none other than the Master of Massey College himself. The page-flipping noises—mysteriously amplified as only the sounds of otherworldly spirits can be—were generated by the ghost rifling through a Folio Society edition of *The Deptford Trilogy*.

Now, I have a skeptical bent, and therefore never rule out *anything* altogether, but before that night, I would have rated the possibility of finding Robertson Davies sitting at my dining table reading a volume of Robertson Davies a definite long shot.

Davies did not seem to notice my entrance. Or if he did, he cared not at all. He sat and read, and chuckled and nodded, until finally I felt like some introductions were in order.

"May I help you?" I asked, immediately regretting it, for it sounded simultaneously rude and unsuitably pedestrian for the occasion.

"Well, I'm glad to see you have at least one volume of quality in this drafty little house," he said, his fiery eyes finally looking up to meet mine.

Now, I pride myself on my humility. If, for instance, one is to point out that I run a little to the heavy side, or that the pitch of my voice can sometimes rise to an unmanly alto, I simply chuckle and say "too true" and am no worse for it. And I am certainly not known for my steely resolve in the face of the supernatural. But no one, whether of this world, or the next, comes to my house and belittles my collection of books.

"No doubt, it is meager by your standards," I said levelly, "but what you see here is merely a portion of the Pettigrew collection. Besides, if you had bothered to look for anything besides your own picture on the dust jacket, you might have concluded differently."

At this, the Master stood up violently, knocking over the chair upon which he sat and rising to his full height—his full immortal height, that is, of at least eight or nine feet by my reckoning. This was impressive, given the seven-foot ceilings in my house. Perhaps he shrunk me at the same time.

⚔ *Christmas Stalkings* ⚔

Todd Pettigrew

"And what," he boomed, "have you to boast of lining these flimsy shelves?"

Somehow my soul held firm.

"The shelves may be modest," I retorted, "but if a fool judges a book by its cover, only a great fool judges a book by what it sits upon."

For a moment I fully expected the spirit of Robertson Davies to destroy me with a blast of flame or a bolt of thunder, but he stared at me for a moment, and then began to laugh. The laugh was good-natured and hearty — so much so that it shook the house to its foundations.

"Well said," he replied, and strolled out of the dining room and into the living room where the Christmas tree glowed and a fire burned steadily and low in the wood stove.

"Ah," he said, regarding the stove wistfully, "a Yuletide fire is the one thing that still makes me long for mortality."

Then his smile faded, and he turned to me with a countenance that had become stern once more.

"I suppose you wonder why I have come to you like this?"

"The question did make the agenda," said I.

"My message is simple and easy to understand."

I grimaced at the implication that I would not be able to follow a more complex message, but this time I held my tongue.

"I simply mean to tell you that you must cancel next week's event — this so-called Gaudy — and its readings."

"You want me to cancel a reading of your stories?" I asked. "But why?"

"Why?" he said. "You answer your own question. Those stories are *mine*."

"Well, yes," I countered. "And we have credited you fully. You appear quite handsomely on the posters."

"Still, they are mine and you did not so much as ask my permission to read them."

🍂 *Christmas Stalkings* 🍂

A Chat with the Master

"Permission? But, with respect, I would have supposed that you were, well, beyond asking."

"All the more reason to let my stories be. Let them rest in peace, like their author."

"Their author has not extended me the same courtesy," I mumbled, glancing at the clock.

"What was that?" said Davies.

"Uh," I said, "their author could now extend that same courtesy." I thought I saw where this was going. "Professor Davies, I would hereby like to formally request your consent to read publicly from the volume known as *High Spirits* at this gathering and at subsequent similar gatherings. In short, sir, may we have your permission?"

I felt sure this request and its elegant phrasing would resolve the matter. The old ghost's pride had been wounded and he longed, it seemed to me, once more to be treated like a living author.

He smiled warmly once again. "No."

"But why not?" I cried, for by this point I had more or less lost my fear of the ghost and was speaking to the Master man to man, as it were. "People have really appreciated them. You should have seen the crowd that gathered last year. And it brings joy to people at this most joyful time of year. And besides, the proceeds go to the public lib—"

I had overplayed my hand, for I knew what the Master thought on this subject.

"To the library? A public library?" he roared. "I assumed that at the very least this travesty was for the benefit of your local university. "But a man who gets all his books at a public library—"

"Yes, I know, ought to get all his meals—"

"At a soup kitchen," the ghost finished for me.

"Well we don't have soup kitchens anymore," I said, "or not very many. We have food banks. And that position

Todd Pettigrew

always seemed rather mean-spirited to me. And besides, what do you care? You're dead. You're not missing out on any royalties."

"It goes beyond that, my boy," said the ghost. "There is a principle involved." And he sat down on an armchair, staring once again at the fire.

"Well, don't sulk," I chided him. "It's unbecoming a ghost of your stature."

"Humbug."

"And besides," I said, for I was growing anxious and did not much like the thought of my wife coming home expecting a hot bath in the tub and finding instead a heated phantom in the drawing room. "You are no longer a person. You can't sue us, and unless you have some powers that you have not shown, you are physically incapable of stopping me from doing as I please."

The ghost glared at this outrage.

"Hell," I said, "next year we might start into the *Marchbanks Diaries*!"

"I may not be able to stop you," he said. "But I can do worse. I can haunt you!"

"Go ahead!" I shot back, "My wife is a licensed real estate salesperson and she assures me that a famous ghost doubles the value of any home. It's better than a swimming pool and sea view combined!"

"Tactless imbecile!" shouted Davies.

"Feckless spectre!" I shouted back.

We continued in this vein for some time. At last, we both seemed to run out of insults.

"Enough of this," he said finally. "You are a professor of literature and one of the few who has not subscribed to the hateful post-modern theory that has declared the author dead."

"Not dead enough," I murmured, but Davies took no note.

"I demand that you, as a fellow Man of Letters, respect my authorial intent."

I almost relented. I almost agreed simply to be done with this spiritual fiasco. But then a thought occurred.

"Is there," I inquired, "no mechanism in the other realm to resolve such disputes?"

"Mechanism?" Davies responded with a glint of something that resembled apprehension in his ethereal eye.

"Yes," I said, emboldened by this first sign of weakness. "Some sort of arbitration where souls of good conscience, incarnate or not, can resolve their differences?"

The ghost paled, which I did not think possible. "Oh, now you've done it," he cried. "You've called for formal mediation!"

"And what's wrong with that?"

"What's wrong," wailed the ghost, "is that according to the laws of our world, the Highest Spirits will appoint an arbitrator."

"Good," I said. "Just what I want."

"So you say. But the Highest Spirits have a way of choosing the most vexing of arbitrators. I would not be surprised if they sent—"

Here he broke off as the door of the wood stove flew open and, with a great bellow of flame, smoke, and steam, a massive figure appeared and took form.

He was an old man and yet strangely familiar. In fact, he looked as though he could be...

"Hello, Father," said Robertson Davies, grimly.

"Hello, my son," said William Rupert Davies.

Rupert Davies was, in his day, a famous newspaper man, and was appointed to the Senate by MacKenzie King. This knowledge filled me with joy, for if there is any body in Canada legitimately famous for its efficiency and fairness, it is the Senate of Canada.

Todd Pettigrew

The details of the mediation need not detain us here. As Shakespeare said, 'tis long to tell and tedious to hear.' Suffice it to say that Davies the Elder proved a delight. His Welsh-inflected speech was beautifully elegant and he proved himself a much better listener than his son. He took care to understand both sides of the argument and to neither show favouritism to the scion of the house of Davies, nor to chide him too much as a patriarch.

Finally, the grand old man of the Red Chamber was ready to issue his ruling.

The stories, he said, did belong, at least morally, to his son. On the other hand, his son had indeed shuffled off the mortal coil of copyright, and the world should not be deprived of the joy that comes from hearing such stories well read.

"And yet," said Rupert Davies, "your readings have already consumed six of the fourteen stories in question. You have assigned two more to your fellow readers for this year — thus using up more than half of the *High Spirits* tales. You would soon be out of stories anyway."

Robertson Davies nodded and a smile played over his translucent visage.

"Therefore," the old Senator concluded, "I will allow the reading of two more tales at your event this year. But," he intoned, raising a hand to silence his son, "you may read no more."

"No more," I cried. "So this year's event is to be our last?"

"Not at all," said the old Senator. "No one, not even my son, owns the idea of a Christmas ghost tale. If they did, he would have had to answer to the Ghost of Dickens years ago."

Robertson Davies looked abashed at this. "Humbug," he said again.

"Continue your annual night of stories," the Old Senator continued, "but, in future, make the stories your own."

⚜ *Christmas Stalkings* ⚜

A Chat with the Master

I had to agree the judgement seemed fair.

"What's more," said the Senator, "our appearance here tonight will furnish a modest tale to get you started. Everyone, of course, will think you made it up, but that is part of the fun. Indeed, we ghosts deliberately behave strangely just to throw mortals off the track."

With this, the elder spirit rose, bowed gracefully, said goodnight, and vanished into the still open wood stove. Robertson Davies nodded curtly and then gave me a look which seemed to say that he would be watching from not too far away and, he too, vanished in the manner of his father.

And as though it had never happened, the house was as it had been before.

I returned upstairs, followed by my tribe of cats who had, apparently, slept through the whole thing. I replaced my copy of *High Spirits* on the shelf. "The Ghost Who Would Not Circulate" would not be read this year.

I sat down at my desk, and began to write.

Author Notes

When it became apparent that we would soon run out of Robertson Davies stories to read at our annual event, the idea of writing our own original tales seemed increasingly sensible, if not unavoidable. But moving from all-Davies one year to no-Davies the next seemed artless and might have been confusing to our small number of loyal attendees.

Christmas Stalkings

Todd Pettigrew

Thus it occurred to me to finish an evening with one original story that proposed the future plan and gave a spiritually compelling reason for it. And who better to appear as a ghost than the man whose spirits had inspired us in the first place?

Ken Chisholm

Joyce to the World

O f course it would be Christmas Eve when my life would be upended by a visitor from the supernatural realm.

Besides the most famous example of a Yuletide haunting recounted by the great Dickens, I had three years' experience of attendance at the Gaudy Night readings at the McConnell Branch of our Regional Library. These tales of the unexplainable in the cozy and bookish rooms of colleges and academics should have been warning enough. But no—I tucked myself in bed that evening, blissfully beyond suspicion of the spectral crisis soon to confront me.

Inerasable memories from my childhood always came to mind on this particular evening. Memories of Roman Catholic catechism class—or as I somehow remembered it: "cataclysm class"—presided over by Sister Mary Jude Dominica Every December, on the last day before the Christmas holiday, she retold the story of how the beasts sharing the stable with the infant Jesus received the miraculous gift of speech at the stroke of midnight. And because it was a Roman Catholic gift, it was a miracle with a sharp edge as Sister Mary Jude Dominica reminded my classmates, "If a human being, even an ignorant dirty little one like the lot of you, were to hear one single syllable uttered by these blessed beasts, you would drop dead on the spot and be shipped off to Purgatory to work off the heinous load of sins you have ungratefully soiled your immortal souls with. Right, boy-os?"

"Yes, Sister Mary Jude Dominica," we dutifully replied.

But despite all of my foreknowledge of the supernatural powers gathered around Christmas, I still was completely unprepared for the threat already secretly at work in my home.

As you will see, I blame this disaster on my cat, because, as a rule, cats are to blame for every disaster, particularly those involving the supernatural. Cats, by instinct, are attracted to the supernatural as they are to an open can of tuna fish.

Roxie, my brown, male, tiger-striped tabby, was still in the throes of feline adolescence. He had resolved that his favourite toy was gravity: with the flick of his paw, he would knock anything he found on a table top or bookshelf or microwave over the edge and onto the floor. Shopping bags, he decided, were also for knocking over and burrowing into for anything edible.

At night, he would dash through my apartment like a furry pyroclastic cloud before leaping onto my bed and prodding my face as an invitation to get up and play at this unsaintly hour of the night.

That night, almost one full year ago, though, I was serenely asleep in my bed, contentedly dreaming of Christmas Day turkey dinner at my sister's home, and indulging in a second (or maybe it was a third) helping of the two types of dressing she thoughtfully provided.

Somewhere, a clock tolled the midnight hour. I did not hear through my slumbers, but Roxie, ears aquiver, must have because he reacted to the distant sound as if it was a starter's pistol.

Off he ran and, like a guided missile, threw himself at a shopping bag full of books, sending them across the floor of my living room. I woke at the "Mrrrhr?" Roxie queried of the mess he had created.

"Hello," a soft, lilting male voice replied.

Joyce to the World

That startled me into sudden wakefulness. I had an intruder in my apartment.

Shoving my feet into my slippers, grabbing my robe, I rushed into my living room only to behold the most eerie, most bone-chilling, most perplexing sight I had ever seen.

A dull green light suffused the length of my living room, casting a ghost-like pallor on my few sticks of furniture and the multitude of books lining the walls, precariously piled on every available flat surface including chairs, tables, and much of the floor space. A low moaning drone hung in the air like the sound from a mossy bagpipe inflated from the lungs of a tubercular baboon.

The glow seemed to emanate from the male form standing at the center of the room, which I perceived to be slightly bent over, gently stroking Roxie's fur, who reciprocated by rubbing his flank against the man's trousered leg.

He was tallish, slim, had a thin moustache. He wore a light-coloured suit and tie showing signs of age, a wide brimmed hat, thick black-rimmed glasses, and held in his hand, to my eyes at the time, a formidable walking stick. In my half-drowsy state, he looked very familiar, but—no, it couldn't be. There was no way *he* should be standing in my living room.

Roxie, seeing my arrival, ceased his rare bout of sustained purring and bounded to where I stood; not, I must add, from a genuine affection, but in the expectation of being fed. "Who are you?" I tremulously asked the glowing man, "and what are you doing in my living room?"

"A living room," the man said in a thoughtful manner. I detected what sounded to my drowsy ears something of an Irish accent. "Living…Livia…Livia plume…a livia plume…a livia plum…better," he said, in a low, contemplative voice. "Would you be kind enough to loan me a pencil and scrap of paper, sir?"

Ken Chisholm

Well, at least now I knew what he was doing in my living room: composing forced, vaguely-literary puns. But he had not answered my first question, so I repeated it.

"Excuse me, sir, I am James Joyce, and you are the one who summoned me," he replied, bowing slightly.

Okay, the glowing green entity claimed to be James Joyce, author of *Ulysses*, my absolute favourite novel, and by some unknown process he stood in my living room at midnight Christmas Eve accusing me...me!...of conjuring him as if I possessed the abilities of some sort of cunning man.

The only thing that convinced me I was not actually dreaming were the painful pricks of Roxie's claws as they

Joyce to the World

dug through the thin fabric of my pajama legs and into the vulnerable goose bumps of my flesh.

The pain focussed my thoughts: for the first time, I noticed the sprawl of books spreading from the large Sobey's shopping bag Roxie had knocked over in his midnight sprint.

I recognized most of its contents. I had crammed nearly three dozen books into this bag during the final day of the library's late November book sale. On that day, one could purchase for just five dollars whatever one could fit into one shopping bag. For a bibliophile like myself, it was like having another Christmas. And having worked in three bookstores in my lifetime, I have acquired the ability to cram the maximum number of books in any size space the way a Prime Minister can pack the Senate.

But one bulky tome lying prostrate on the top of the pile, I definitely had no recollection of finding at the McConnell book sale: a vintage hardcover edition of *Finnegans Wake* — the final masterwork of language created by the living embodiment of the sickly green shade that stood before me.

Although I was more a fan of *Ulysses*, the other enormous novel of Joyce's that covered one ordinary day in the lives of Dubliners, I had been on the hunt for a hardcover copy of the *Wake* to complete my collection of Joyce's works. They were hard to come by in anything close to my price range. How I could have discovered one at the McConnell book sale and not noticed it defied explanation. Even in the hurly-burly of five dollar a bag day — which made T-bone time at the tiger cage resemble tea time at Buckingham Palace — I would have paused long enough to exult over my find.

"This is your novel," I said to the spectral Joyce.

"It is," the shade replied with a certain smugness. "You've heard of it."

"Oh, yes," I said, compelled to examine it both as a printed treasure but also because a premonition gnawed at my

Christmas Stalkings

fevered imagination this book must have had something to do with the arrival of my ghostly visitor.

"Excuse me for just one sec," I said.

"Await your pleasure," the shade said amiably. Too amiably, if I had been paying closer attention.

Tentatively, I picked up the book: it felt surprisingly warm in my trembling hands.

It was a first edition of the British Faber and Faber 1939 edition, regular trade edition, the dust jacket design familiar from its use on later paperback editions. Inside, the pages gleamed like fresh cream in sunlight. Remarkably for a first edition of the *Wake*, all of the leaves had been cut, suggesting at least one of its owners had actually finished the notoriously difficult text.

I checked the title page and there — again I could hardly believe my eyes — was Joyce's signature in his famously preferred green ink under a dedication: "For my beautiful scourge, Madame Zukov. May your desires be my desires." It was dated: December 24, 1940, Zurich — just weeks before Joyce's death from an unsuccessful ulcer operation. Under this odd inscription were three red brown blotches like small representations of exploding stars.

I was holding in my unbelieving hands a book worth thousands, if not tens of thousands, of dollars.

"And would that be enough to purchase me a small glass of wine?" the apparition spoke in a quiet lilt.

I reddened when I realized I had spoken aloud.

"My apologies, sir…Mr. Joyce," I stammered. "I don't have any wine in the house."

"Whiskey? No? Brandy? No? Beer? Ah, another teetotaller," the ghostly Joyce sighed.

"I'm sorry," I said weakly, "I am an enormous fan, though—"

"Of course, you are." The spectre had the most enchanting Dublin accent. His ectoplasmic presence suddenly sharpened and grew brighter. "You've read the *Wake*?"

"Oh, of course, but *Ulysses*—" I began.

"You never finished it, did you?" the ghost grew slightly dimmer.

"I'm afraid not—"

If it was possible to sadden a poor creature already quite dead, I had managed the feat.

"How far?" he looked at me. "How far did you manage?'

"Page fourteen?" I replied.

The ghost sighed and my living room took on a sudden chill.

"It is a tough read," I said, feeling defensive. "Didn't you put in so many enigmas and puzzles that it would keep the professors busy arguing for centuries over what you meant?"

"I said that about *Ulysses*," the ghost said, and then breathed a heartfelt moan. "I also said that's the only way of insuring one's immortality. Ah, Madam Zukov, you beautiful, cruel—"

"Who is Madame Zukov?" I ventured.

"The original purchaser of that copy of my work in progress," the shade replied. "She was another 'enormous fan' of my work," he said with a slight wrinkle of distaste. "But unlike some, being a well-travelled, polyglot charlatan dealing in credulous occultists, she sped through the entire work in under a week. She tracked me down in Zurich and cornered me in a pastry shop and accused me of plagiarizing from her pamphlet on how she communicated with the spirits of the murdered Romanovs—"

"Did you—plagiarize her, I mean?"

"Of course, I did," Joyce's shade replied, his exasperation getting the better of him. "Have you not read my books like you said? I take commonplace idiocies and make it part of a

Ken Chisholm

greater work. Her impertinence caused my ulcer to flare in agony. I told her it would immortalize her along with me. I had done her a favour. Her whole book was ill-composed nonsense. She said so was my work: without plot or characters or anything to hold a reader's interest—as if I had an interest in achieving any of those commonplaces. And she said my Norwegian puns were not funny. In her agitation, she let her accent slip and I had her. I said my books were not meant for upstart Donegal girls who, because they were dancing around the Lughnasa fire one day and pretending to talk to dead Russian royalty the next, were not fit judges of the quality of my work, especially the *Wake*. Then she said she wished I stayed on Earth long enough to hear someone read the *Wake* cover to cover so I could hear what a rotten piece of work it was."

"She cursed you!" I exclaimed.

"I did that myself with that ill-advised dedication," he said.

"After all that, you signed her copy?" I asked.

"She did buy it and read it, after all," the shade said. "But she sealed the invocation by pricking my hand with her hatpin and drawing three drops of my blood before I had a chance to defend myself. You must be on guard always around those Donegal County creatures, especially when their blood is up."

"That was over seventy years ago!" I said. "And you have found no-one to read—"

"Many have professed their love of my books, all have promised to deliver me from my torment," he fixed me with a mournful look that broke my heart, "but in the end, all have disappointed and betrayed me. You will be no different."

Along with the sting of the passive-aggressive insult to my character, I felt empathy for my personal author hero trapped in literary limbo. And furthermore — and this was the clincher — it was Christmas!

"I'll do it," I said, tightening the sash of my robe. "We'll start right now."

"You're familiar with the *Wake*?"

"Not entirely, but I've read *Dubliners* — "

"The cat could read *Dubliners*," Joyce's shade said, to which Roxie assented with a thoughtful meow.

"And the *Portrait of the Artist* — "

"And could follow all of the Latin theological allusions — "

"And *Ulysses*: more than once!"

"With a scholarly gloss in your hand each time, no doubt."

"Well, if I'm not good enough, you can always hope Madame Zukov will rescind her curse."

Joyce's shade sighed. "Let us begin." And he sat down next to me on my couch.

I opened the book. I must admit to feeling a delicious expectation: I saw myself and Joyce enjoying convivial nightly reading sessions as we slowly but steadily made our way through the *Wake*.

Yes, it had no real plot except a kind of dream-logic one. Yes, its characters kept changing their names and identities and how many of them there were. Yes, it may be the dream of Humphrey Childers Earwicker ruminating over some indecent, even incestuous, act he was caught performing in a Dublin park. Yes, Joyce chose to tell this thin tale in hundreds of thousands of puns, portmanteau words, mash-up free associations drawn from over six languages.

I could feel my resolve dissolving. No. I gave my word. Onward.

But a malicious voice in my head reminded me, *He puns in Norwegian*.

Joyce's shade impatiently shifted on the couch where he sat.

❧ *Christmas Stalkings* ❧

My resolve re-resolved: Joyce, the *Wake*, months of fun. Better than having cable TV.

"'riverrun, past Eve and Adam's—'"

"What are you doing?" the shade asked testily.

"Reading the first sentence," I said. "'...from swerve of shore to bend of bay—'"

Joyce's shade put his ectoplasmic hands up to cover his ghostly ears.

"Whatever accent you are affecting to read in, please desist," he said.

"I'm not affecting any accent," I protested. "That's how I normally speak."

"There is nothing normal about that accent," Joyce said.

I wanted to protest that it was a perfectly acceptable Cape Breton accent but Joyce's shade cut me off.

"The *Wake* needs to be heard spoken in a proper Dublin accent," Joyce said. "Otherwise, the word play doesn't work."

"'riverrun'," I tried again, imitating Joyce's accent.

"That is the accent of a music hall Irish washerwoman," Joyce said. "Listen to me."

I listened. I followed his every inflection. It was a disaster.

"Raheefurruin, pahst Eff and Edam's," was the closest I came before he stopped me again.

Wearily, Joyce's shade said, "Listen. Repeat. Like a gramophone. And stop thinking."

Five hours later or so, I had read the opening sentence to Joyce's satisfaction. I knew it had taken several hours because I could feel the bristles of my beard rising on my cheeks.

It occurred to me the sun should be glimmering through my east facing living room window, but outside it remained pitch black. I looked at the wall clock over my desk. With horror, I saw its two hands frozen upright, as if in prayer, still proclaiming it to be not quite one minute after midnight. It was silent, too: its familiar *tick tock* eerily stilled.

Christmas Stalkings

Joyce to the World

"What did you do to my clock?"

"Nothing," Joyce's shade said. "It will continue to function...when we have finished reading the *Wake*."

"You've stopped time!"

"A providential side consequence of the curse," he said, a slight smile at the corners of his mouth, "so we can't be interrupted."

"But I'll be in my eighties by the time we get through this thing!" I sputtered.

"It's nothing I would not ask of any of my readers, especially my 'enormous fans'," he added as his smile broadened into a wolfish grin.

At that moment, a cold chill shook my entire frame. Along with the comprehension of the fiendish plot I had fallen into. I also remembered another famous quotation attributed to the living Joyce: "The demand that I make of my reader is that he should devote his whole life to reading my works."

"You tricked me!" I said.

"You haven't spent seven decades in limbo," he replied coolly.

"This deal is off."

"Our deal is only over when you finish reading the *Wake*," Joyce's shade said, making himself more comfortable on the couch. "Come, sir, we have at least another five hundred pages to enjoy."

He had me foxed. I could think of no way to extricate myself.

"Merm," Roxie said from where he lay on the floor. During our reading session, he had amused himself by batting his paws at the heap of books that had shared the shopping bag with the *Wake*.

"Not now, animal," I said, in my misery.

Ken Chisholm

"Marmerrmar," the cat replied. My eyes fell upon him and how he was flicking through what should have been a Penguin edition of Martin Chuzzlewit.

Only its pages were as blank as a newly purchased journal. Odd. *Wait a sec...that coffee table book of classic Hollywood movies is also open, and its pages are blank, too.*

I grabbed other books from the pile: each of them had nothing but blank pages.

"What did you do to my books?" I demanded of Joyce's shade.

"I read them all. Or something like that," he replied. "Then I had to find a space for them to fit in this copy of the *Wake*. I didn't finish that task until this evening. Now, if we are to start again from the beginning…"

It was at that moment our eyes locked and Joyce's shade knew this jig was up.

"Time to get back in your bottle, genie-us," I said, grabbing an armful of books from a nearby chair and throwing them into the shopping bag.

"Traitor!" Joyce's shade cried.

"You should have stopped after *Ulysses*," I said, slamming shut the cover of the *Wake* like a prison cell door and blithely tossing it into the shopping bag.

As soon as it made contact with the jumble of books, Joyce's shade gave an inhuman shriek, with a charming Irish lilt, and quickly dissolved into a pus-green cloud of smoke that funnelled itself into the shopping bag. I speedily piled as many books as I could on top of it.

Joyce read St. Augustine and Dante, but he had a compulsion to read everything; dime novels, city street gazettes, old racing papers, anything that could enhance his own work. I knew as long as I fed him a steady diet of books, I could keep his spirit, and our pact, at bay.

Joyce to the World

And so it was for Christmas and the New Year and to February when, for his birthday on the second, I gave him some Thomas Pynchon and Don DeLillo. That quieted him almost until June 15, Bloomsday, the day on which *Ulysses* is set. By then I was shovelling in anything I could find: the Cape Breton telephone directory, some Sears' catalogues, pamphlets on avoiding sexually transmitted diseases. On occasion, when murmurs of revolt came from the shopping bag, I simply waved something from the collected works of Dan Brown and the smell of it shut him up real quick.

But this was only a temporary reprieve. I had to get Joyce's shade and his print prison out of the apartment.

I always said if I think long and hard about something, eventually the obvious will occur to me.

So a couple of weeks ago on the first Saturday in December, I brought the haunted copy of the *Wake* to the five-dollar-a-bag day ending the latest McConnell fundraising book sale. I am gratified to see many of you who attended that last day of the sale are in attendance at tonight's performance.

In fact, it may even have been your recklessly unattended bag into which I slipped the cursed copy of the *Wake*. In the bustle and frenzy of the sale, even I had trouble remembering in whose bag I secreted the great book.

No matter. Christmas Eve is nigh and no doubt it will become clear into whose possession I passed my treasure.

But I have generously given you all the information you need to survive your encounter with Joyce's shade. Or, you could prove yourself the world's greatest Joyce reader.

Either way, make sure to get your own damn cat.

To everybody else, I wish a happy and Joyce-less Christmas.

Christmas Stalkings

Ken Chisholm

Author Notes

At the first Gaudy Night reading at the McConnell, I was a very entertained audience member. The second year, Todd Pettigrew, the event's organiser, asked me, as the Cape Breton Regional Library's Storyteller in Residence, to read one of Davies' stories which I happily agreed to do. After that event he brought up the idea that we should compose our own tales — to which I remember answering with a confident, "Yes?"

In both stories I eventually contributed, I made the deliberate decision to incorporate actual events and services I had used at the McConnell.

The haunted copy of *Finnegans Wake* (the story contains much of the actuality of my James Joyce fanboy devotion) came from the highly anticipated and enthusiastically attended twice-yearly book sale at the McConnell. Knowing that a sizable portion of my audience would have attended it, I decided to include them in the story. Did they unknowingly take home a haunted book? Nah-ha-ha-ha!

Todd Pettigrew

The Ghost who came to Visit for a Spell

Last year at this time, I told you the story of my singular encounter with the ghost of Robertson Davies and how I had promised that majestic spectre that this year would feature new stories along the same lines. At the time, standing as I was with that formidable spirit, the prospect of meeting ghosts seemed not at all implausible. If you had asked me, I would have confidently predicted a veritable parade of apparitions in the coming months, all providing me with material for no end of tales, of yarns. Perhaps even a ballad or two.

But the new year came without the hint of a ghost. No phantom threatened my Valentine's Day. Easter came without anyone rising from the dead. Well, no one recently, I mean. And so the year went. Summer passed without paranormal incident and autumn was mellow and fruitful, not hellish and spook-filled.

And so, as the snows of December started to swirl, a chilling thought came upon me. What if I remain entirely unhaunted? Shall I have to stoop to *inventing* a story? Davies would never have done such a thing! The thought was more terrifying than any ghost could ever have been.

But the thought had scarcely taken up residence in my mind when an event occurred that nearly made me wish such contrivance had been necessary.

It was a cold night—for, as you know, the weather has been uncharacteristically harsh this Yuletide, and I was grading exam papers at my dining room table as is my normal custom at this time of year. This was a particularly uninspired batch of tests and so the red ink flowed almost as freely as the invective and craft beer. I had just put my favourite Christmas CD — *Barenaked for the Holdiays* — in the player and started those jaunty tunes going, when out of the corner of my eye, I spied a boy, perhaps eleven or twelve, standing in the room with me.

I knew him at once to be a ghost. Not only did he exhibit a tell-tale translucence, but his clothes were not of this era. His entire demeanor placed him, to my untrained eye, almost a century in the past. He appeared dirty and thin, but generally in good health. Dead, obviously, but besides that, in fine form. And there was something familiar in his posture, as though I had seen other children standing just as he was now.

Now, I should have been polite. Not only was he a child, and a guest of a kind, but he was also the ghost I had been hoping for nearly a year, would arrive. But as you will recall, I was up to my neck in amateur analysis of poetry and in a bad mood.

"And what do you want?" I asked, my voice surly.

"I'm ready for my first word," he replied calmly.

This took me aback. "What word?"

"The first word I am to spell."

It took me a moment, but my exam-addled brain cleared and I deduced what he was looking for.

At this point I must explain to those who don't know me that among my many tasks as a professor of English, I am sometimes called upon to serve as an official at spelling bees. In fact, I am something of a celebrity in the fast-paced world of competitive orthography.

"You've come to spell words," I said.

"Yes," he replied, "and I intend to win."

Christmas Stalkings

The Ghost who came to Visit for a Spell

"Well, you've come too early," I said. "The Nova Scotia spelling bee is still two months away. You'll have to come back then."

"I'm ready now," he insisted. "My first word, please."

"Oh very well," I said. And just to make him feel like he was doing well, I gave him an easy one.

"Jeopardy."

"You need the bell," he intoned brightly.

"The bell?"

"In case I get one wrong. You have to ring the bell."

There are, I would imagine, only a handful people in this world who can put their hands on a spelling bee bell at a moment's notice. I happen to be one of them. I obliged. His pessimism over the expectation that I might need the bell was heartening, and I began to imagine how this little adventure would play out. I would give him a word or two, he would misspell soon enough, I would hit the dreaded bell and he would be free to continue his long overdue journey to the next world.

With said bell installed on my dining table, the ghost seemed satisfied.

"Would you repeat the word, please?"

"Jeopardy," I said again.

He smiled and gave the correct spelling without so much as a shaking hand or troubled brow. "Next word."

"Psalm," I said, hoping to trip him up with the silent P. But he rattled it off without error. I should have been looking to extend his visit, but having no children of my own, I sometimes find young people unnerving, and I had forgotten how intimidating it can be to stand in the presence of disembodied souls. In a word, I was restless. It was time to turn up the lexicographical heat.

Todd Pettigrew

Christmas Stalkings

The Ghost who came to Visit for a Spell

"Pulchritude," I said, expecting him to at least be given pause. He was not. My mind searched for harder and harder words. "Harridan," I tried next. No dice. This was getting serious.

"Hypobulia," I intoned, knowing this was a champion speller's word.

He didn't miss a beat.

Hamadryad. Syzygy. Weimaraner. He spelled them all flawlessly.

"How do you know so many words?" I finally cried out — losing for the first time the professional decorum that has earned me so much regard among spelling bee judges.

"I have been studying for nearly a century," he said proudly. "Beneath this very spot, in fact."

"Beneath?" I stammered.

And then multiple realizations dawned at once. My house, as is common in Glace Bay where I live, sits atop long abandoned mine shafts. And I also recalled from a visit to my local miner's museum that the old mines used to employ young boys to open and close doors for ventilation.

Enticing the lad into conversation — a welcome relief from spelling — I eventually learned that my young visitor was just such a boy as my tour guides had spoken of. From what I could gather, he had been an exceedingly bright child in school, but when his father broke his leg in a man-rake accident, the boy, whose name was Jeremiah, as it happened, agreed to go underground to assure the family at least a meager income while his father was laid up. His mother, saddened at the prospect of her precocious son's studies being choked off in this way, secured for him the only book that she could find that she knew to be suitable for learning. A tattered old Webster's dictionary she found at a flea market. It was his present for the Christmas of 1924.

Todd Pettigrew

"You learn all dem words," his mother told Jeremiah, "and then you kin make up any other book you want."

Jeremiah lasted all of two weeks in the pit before the cave in. He died, even as thousands of other children were preparing for the first ever Scripps National Spelling Bee.

But while his body lay beneath the earth like so many others, his soul persevered. And he remained there year after year, decade upon decade, studying his dictionary, learning every word there was to learn. Until by whatever turning of whatever cosmic wheels bring mortal men and immortal spirits together, he had come to me. Come to show what he had learned. Come to do his mother proud.

I gave him his next word. And a word after that. And another.

And so it went for hours.

I grew increasingly desperate. With no other competitors, there was no way for Jeremiah to win. But with his superhuman knowledge of the dictionary, there was no way for him to lose. He simply knew every word there was.

Then a thought occurred. He knew every word there *was*. In 1924. Jeremiah's dictionary would have stopped before 1924, and so I only needed to give him a word from later than that period and he would be stumped.

It shouldn't be too hard, I thought. New words come into the language every day. Though fatigue had worn me down, I knew I must rally. I took a deep breath and was about to resume.

Looking into Jeremiah's dark, hopeful eyes, I felt bad for what I was about to do. To dash a centuries worth of hopes, that for which he had worked his whole life — well afterlife, technically — to achieve seemed cruel.

"Come on, you round old fool," said the child impatiently, "get on with it."

Suddenly my plan seemed less cruel.

Christmas Stalkings

The Ghost who came to Visit for a Spell

"Airplane," I said

To my surprise, the boy chuckled, and spelled A E R O P L A N E. I cursed inwardly. My word was not quite modern enough. His spelling was a bit archaic, but I had to accept it nevertheless.

But I took comfort. My plan was still sound. I just needed a thoroughly modern word.

"Podcast," I said.

For the first time that evening I saw a flicker of discomfort pass over the young man's ghostly countenance.

"Definition?" he said for the first time.

"An electronic recording made freely available via the Internet," I said with a smile.

He looked away as his mind pored over the P section of the old dictionary that he had laboriously stored in his... brain? In any case, he paused, looked back at me and I saw his eyes narrow. He had realized what I was doing and clearly thought it to be foul play, but he also knew there was nothing he could do about it.

With a sigh of determination, not despair, he fell back on the oldest trick in the spelling bee book. He spelled it as it sounded.

"P O D C A S T."

By Dickens' ghost! I thought. *I will never be rid of this spirit.* I pictured an eternity of Jeremiah following me around while I repeated every word in the language over and over until my own death released me. The prospect was nothing short of a living hell.

But no, I was not to be so easily defeated by this pint-sized poltergeist. There were plenty of modern words. Surely one would trip him up.

Overkill. A simple compound of words an infant could spell. *RADAR* — too phonetic. Even *petrichor* — the smell in the air shortly after it begins to rain—he deduced from its Greek roots.

The fire had burned low, my brain had grown tired, and even the Barenaked Ladies had finished their final chorus of the Dreidel song. But I needed words! *Dreidel*? No. *Compact disc?* No. Some component perhaps—*maybe, could he?*—I had to try.

Somehow, deep in my soul I knew this was my last hope. If Jeremiah spelled this word correctly, I knew I would be haunted by him forever.

I took another long inhalation. And I pronounced the fateful word.

"Laser."

Jeremiah stared at me intently. Somewhere in his encyclopedic mind, a warning flag was going up. He knew it might not be as easy as it sounded. He asked all the questions—origin, definition, part of speech, if I could repeat the word? A flicker of optimism lit within me. I had seen this before. He was stalling. And yet, he hadn't missed yet.

Finally he took the plunge and began.

"L A..."

He paused as I have heard so many before him do when they come to a tricky spot. The fateful letter—what was it?

"Z E R," he finished.

Relief flooded my soul as I reached out and rang the bell. It was over. Jeremiah was out. However, my relief quickly made way for a modicum of sorrow as I saw the disappointment in the boy's face.

"I'm sorry," I said. "But you'll have to go now. Don't worry. I'm sure you're headed to a better place."

"Yes," he returned, stoically, wiping a teary drop of ectoplasm from his eye. "Perhaps you could direct me?"

"Direct you?" I said, astounded. "I'm afraid that's not really my area."

The Ghost who came to Visit for a Spell

"You, a professor of literature? Surely you know where I can find a library?

"A library?"

"Yes, you've made me realize how many new words I must learn in order to compete next year. I must get to a library and learn as much as I can before next year's competition. Where is the nearest one located?"

My friends, I wish I could say that I directed him to the Glace Bay branch of the library not far from where I live, or to the university library where I work. But the truth is that I wanted some distance between me and this ghost, and so I gave him the name of a more...central facility. I mention this only so that you will be prepared when you are browsing the stacks in the coming months.

As for entertaining Jeremiah next year, with time to reflect since the incident, I now believe I hit upon a way to deal with that particular difficulty. For having been born in the year 1912, he will exceed the maximum age requirement by a considerable number of years, and will, sadly, have to be disqualified.

Author Notes

Part of the fun of writing this style of ghost story—for me at least—has been incorporating aspects of my real life into the fantastical, and vice versa. At the time of "A Chat with the Master" I was deeply involved in competitive spelling (as an official) and a ghostly spelling bee seemed like

Todd Pettigrew

an excellent premise. It did mean invoking the notion of a dead child, but the nice thing about fictional ghosts is that we quickly forget about their deaths and see them as characters in their own right.

I am particularly proud of the ending of this one.

Scott Sharplin

No Place Like Home

It scarcely needs to be stated that Christmas, or the holiday season in general, is a time steeped in tradition. Or perhaps "steeped" is the wrong metaphor, for while it might conjure the pleasant yuletide aromas of peppermint tea or nutmeg apple cider, it fails to evoke the discomfort of scalding one's lips by trying to drink said cider through a straw...every year.

Indeed, the discomfort and anxiety that comes from trying to make each year's traditions go without a hitch might lead one to a different idiom. Yet for me to say, "Christmas is lousy with traditions" would be to brand myself a humbug — or a hum-louse? And I freely confess that some traditions bear enough charm to outweigh their impositions.

So, to say that Christmas is a time of baking, of clove-infused craft beer, of voices raised in chorus so as to hide my butchering of lyrics, of witty ghost stories recounted in good company — in these, the Christmas tea is admirably steeped. But insofar as Christmas is a time for shoveling, shopping, hanging lights, and being pestered by the ghosts themselves — it is here that the lice of the season start to crawl across my long-suffering scalp.

It was here in the midst of this precarious balancing act of the heart — poised between festivity and infestation — that I found myself two weeks ago. My teaching term complete, I had thrown myself, perhaps a bit ungently, into yuletide preparations. But I'd failed to factor in the disruptive presence upon my traditions of a boisterous toddler beneath the tinsel. For X (we'll call him X), having been mostly presentient for his first three Xmases, now yearned to put upon all chores his personal stamp—and, of course, when a three-year-old "helps" one with something, one's workload spikes like a heating bill in winter.

So far that day, we'd hung three wreaths, the first two of which lacked the tensile strength to support a toddler's weight; we'd explored the principle of entropy, using several boxes of glass decorations; and we'd hung the outdoor lights—or rather, I hung the lights while X serenaded my labours using my car's alarm fob: "BEEP the BEEP with BEEPs of BEEP—"

After apologizing to the neighbours, we tested out the lights, which led swiftly to another holiday tradition: flipping breakers and re-routing fuses in the basement, while X, unsupervised for less than five minutes, unerringly located all the presents we'd concealed throughout the house. At last, exhausted and still unable to ignite the Christmas lights without denying the microwave its juice, I threw my hands up, and decreed that all traditioning would cease, except for those traditions which involved pyjamas, hot cocoa, and Netflix.

I was, of course, naively optimistic.

So the night found us, father and son, enjoying the 1964 holiday camp classic, Santa Claus Conquers the Martians. And "enjoying" is a stretch—not that there's nothing to enjoy in a film that features an 8-year-old Pia Zadora in bronze body paint singing "Hooray for Santy Claus." But X was nodding off, perhaps done in by the complexities of the plot, and I was preoccupied with another personal end-of-year tradition: despair for the future of mankind.

You cannot tell me I'm alone in this. Black Friday had just come and gone, with its ever-rising toll of frenzied, consumerist self-destruction. The changing climate had recently unleashed the first record-demolishing storm of the season, taking aim at humankind's collective derriere, exposed and hoisted aloft as we kept our head deep in the sand. Even the North Pole, once an idyllic crystalline wonderland reserved for polar bears and magical workshops, seemed on the fast track to becoming the next militarized zone, as all the northern nations desperately laid claim to its oil.

These issues weighed heavily on me, partly because of the extra weight now slumped across my lap, sleeping his way through the third act of Santa's *opus horribilis*. And while my spirits should have been buoyed by my other traditions — even if the outside lights didn't work just yet — I just couldn't muster the cheer. I thought about X's future. *He'll be a grown-up in 2050. Will there be enough energy by then to power a frivolity like Christmas lights? Will his lights flicker in time to a clean, green turbine alongside his energy-efficient house? Or will he use an old string of burnt-out lights to strangle his neighbours over a Christmas can of beans?*

My dread was compounded by a sense of helplessness. I knew the crises, as I catalogued them daily in my head. I knew what sorts of measures I could take to help correct them. And yet, here I was, hanging Christmas lights, planning for another holiday steeped with — *lousy* with — disposable gift-wrap, sweatshop dollar-store plastic gewgaws, and an oven working overtime to cook a turkey, half of which would end up on the floor surrounding X's chair.

Ah, but, I would reason, holidays are the exception! Once a year, Mother Nature will permit me to cut loose. While the rest of the year, I could reassure myself that, as a writer, I was...well, my contributions to these large-scale problems were...um...as a writer...I sometimes buy recycled notebooks ...if they're on sale...

On the screen in front of me, Voldar, the malicious Martian, had just kidnapped Santa Claus — or rather, Dropo, another Martian dressed as Santa Claus. The bronze skin really should have tipped off Voldar.

From behind me, a stentorian voice declared, "This is not how I pictured Mars at all."

My first response, of course, to hearing a strange voice in a dark and empty house, was fear. But that reflex only lasted a heartbeat. Its disruptive arrival into my family room stirred memories, not so much of terror and trauma, but of mild irritation. I had only been visited once before by a ghostly writer at Christmas time, but apparently it was to become a tradition. I made a mental note to investigate the possible causes for this—undigested piece of beef, house constructed on ancient burial site, persuasive academic colleague obsessed with Robertson Davies—and then I sighed, gently adjusted my sleeping filial burden so I could crane my neck to look behind me, and saluted the intrusive spectre.

"Happy Holidays," I said. "I'd offer you some apple cider, but I'm afraid it would go right through you."

My admittedly weak jest was merely dead air to the phantom. It floated haughtily through the sofa, drifting ever closer to the television set. Through the ectoplasmic nimbus that surrounded it, I could make out a heavy-set, middle-aged white man in a tailored three-piece suit. His comb-over and pencil moustache suggested he was of early twentieth century provenance, and his accent placed him in the southern U.K. Those clues, combined with his declared interest in the red planet, prompted me to make an educated guess.

"Herbert Wells, perhaps?"

"Please," he replied with a distracted bow, "everyone calls me H.G."

"This certainly is an honour," I said, forgetting altogether my despair of a few moments past. "You're one of my

No Place Like Home

favourite writers of science fiction—or, do you prefer scientific romance?"

"No matter," said the ghost, turning back to the flickering images of papier-mâché sets and ill-made costumes.

"If it's not an imposition, I have so many questions for you. I'm not even sure where to start. Are you planning to stay awhile?"

"Hmm." The ghost made a noncommittal sound.

I could see that he was becoming hypnotised by the inanities upon the screen, as children or pets sometimes get distracted by flickering lights. I reached for the remote.

"If you're interested in television," I said, "later I could show you some of Neil DeGrasse Tyson's *Cosmos*. But for now—"I clicked off the screen.

"What's all this then?" sputtered the ghost of H.G. Wells. "Reopen the transmission at once. I was just about to get a glimpse of the terrain beyond the walls of Mars' cities."

"Oh!" I said, realizing too late my error. "Forgive me, I should have explained. That screen you see, that's not a live broadcast of anything, thank goodness. That was a fictional performance, like a play, recorded onto film stock and then broadcast—"

"Do not patronize me, sir!" said Wells, prodding the dark flat screen with a luminescent finger. "I may be best remembered for my *fin de siècle* works, but I'll remind you that I clung to this mortal coil until nineteen hundred and forty-six. I saw the fruition of innumerable devices which I, myself, predicted. The moving picture and the electronic television were among the least of my predictions."

"Oh, I know!" I let my inner fanboy out to gush a little bit. "You were a true visionary. Your novels foresaw everything from cell phones to atom bombs. Why, you wrote about genetic engineering in, what was it, 1896?"

Scott Sharplin

"And let us not forget who predicted the outbreak of World War II, with a mere six-month margin of error."

I knew the book that Wells referred to—it was called *The Shape of Things to Come*. But that was written later in his life—in 1933—a time when, in my view, it didn't take a visionary to foresee the war. I was predicting calamity almost daily, and I seemed to be right about half the time. But I let it slide.

Yet in the pause I'd taken to consider this, the ghost had returned his attention yet again to the extinguished television screen. "A pity," He was saying, "I should very much like to see what the cities on Mars look like. Perhaps we have time to hop on a trans-planetary shuttle?"

"Well..." Now we were getting to the downside of the visionary racket: the more futures you predict, the worse your odds for a perfect score. I decided to lie, so as not to bruise his ego. "I'm afraid the shuttles are all closed for the holidays."

The ghost harrumphed. "No matter," he declared. "A quick trip in your time-carriage should resolve that. We can travel a month forward, or in reverse if you prefer. The shuttles would be open then."

"Yes, well...my time-carriage is...in the shop." I shrugged apologetically. "I just don't have the time to fix it. So much to do, you see. The holidays—"

"A pity," said the ghost. "But no surprise. For I also predicted *not having time for things*. It's true. You see, together with my breathtaking visions of limitless mechanical wonder, I saw displeasure as mankind achieved increasing velocities; I saw dismay, dysphoria, and dissonance—all the 'dis' words, really—as we rode the mechanical carousel of our own devise, spinning faster and faster while the world around us is torn up into a discarded, dysfunctional, dys...dys...it's on the tip of my tongue..."

"Dystopia?"

Christmas Stalkings

No Place Like Home

"Precisely! Oh, I was a whiz at dystopias. Barren, post-atomic wastelands, far-flung global garbage heaps, clear-cut and scorched from the heat rays of invading fiends..."

Wells appeared to be getting teary-eyed over his apocalyptic reminiscences. Myself, I could feel despair creeping back in. His descriptions not only evoked the catastrophic futures of *The Time Machine, War of the Worlds* and more; they also reflected the grim imaginings of my own pessimistic mind. As Wells waxed poetic, I flashed back to parking lot riots, and hurricane-force snowstorms, and the international rush for oil beneath the North Pole.

"...the problem, of course, with universal automation is the need for power," Wells was droning on. "And then, should power be cut off, as happens in the future plutocracy of London in *The Sleeper Awakes*, the general population becomes first disoriented, then enraged, then finally — "

"Then finally, they all move to the North Pole!" I snapped, out of patience with the spectre's self-promotion. My admiration for Wells was undiminished, but now my despair was back in full force. As I looked at the man, I saw not a crusader for change, but a powerless pebble in an endless flood. He was a visionary, sure — but as a writer, his job was to foresee dystopias, not to stop them from coming to pass. If such a scribe as H.G. Wells was helpless in the face of progress, what was I? Less than nothing.

Wells regarded me strangely. I regretted my outburst, but before I could apologize, the ghost leaned in and laid an incorporeal, yet somehow still avuncular, hand upon my shoulder. "There, there," he said, stiffly British, yet sincere. "The fault is mine. I became so caught up in my remembrances that I quite forgot why I came."

Strangely perhaps, the question hadn't yet occurred to me, but now it did. I gently shifted so as to let the sleeping three-year-old slump down onto the sofa, then stood up to face the phantom. "Why is that?"

Wells spun his hand in the air mysteriously. "Some benign animus which protects writers must have sensed your despair, and sent me hither from the ether to enliven your spirits."

"Oh," I shrugged, then made my best effort to seem grateful. "That was nice of it."

"I know well the malaise you suffer, sir," said Wells. "It haunted me for much of my young life. But let me chart out my trajectory — for dystopia is only half the story."

With that enigmatic statement, Wells raised his translucent left hand and traced a luminous, straight line across the dark air. The glowing line clung to the air, like headlights in a time-dilated photograph, and I made a mental note to later research the electromagnetic properties of ghosts. Perhaps Wells could help me with my fusebox problem.

"This line represents my life," said Wells. "Eighty years, from 1866 to 1946. Now this line can be taken as an indicator of the general state of happiness in Europe." Reaching back to the first point on his ghostly graph, he traced a second line — not straight this time, but bouncing wildly up and down and with the same unpredictability as one might find in, say, a freelance writer's bank account. Overall, the trend went downwards, with abrupt chasms marking what I figured to be 1914 and 1939. By the end of Wells' timeline, the happiness marker was nearly hitting the hardwood.

"Wait," said Wells. He proceeded to draw a third line. For my sake, I presume, he made each line glow a different colour — red, green, and gold — so that by the end of his work, it felt rather festive in the room. His final line was quite erratic, like the second, yet it appeared almost as a mirror to

No Place Like Home

⚘ *Christmas Stalkings* ⚘

that trend—starting low in the air, and ending up as high as the tall ghost could reach without the aid of levitation. "Behold!" He cried, "My literary arc, from dystopic pessimism to utopian idealism. All those ghastly futures you continue to read and to adapt into your cinematic block-annihilators—they were my early works! The outcomes of my adolescent rebelliousness, my mistrust of authority, and my publisher's preference for cracking-good catastrophe.

"But nearly all my later works—*Days of the Comet, Men Like Gods, The Shape of Things to Come*—predict a future in which mankind bands together in the face of global crisis, overcoming inestimable odds to set the world aright before dystopia descends!"

I stared, bewildered, at the ecto-graph. I understood what Wells was saying, yet it seemed to contradict all reason. "You're telling me that, even as the world descended into war and chaos...as the long shadow of the atom bomb was cast across the continents...you actually became...an optimist?"

Wells spread his hands, as if to say, *There are more things in heaven and earth, Sharplin, than are dreamt of in your philosophy.* His gesture also had the unintended effect of disrupting his glow-chart, dissolving it like sunbeams on a river's surface.

"Chin up, my extant friend. From one writer to another: the future is friendly."

To hear these words coming from the long-dead lips of he who gave us Morlocks, Martian tripods, and the dying Earth of 30 million years AD...it was too much. I began to laugh. This was the last thing I expected after a day of disheartening traditions: a spectral vision that actually cheered me up.

I could tell that Wells was pleased with the success of his mission. "There now, you see? Isn't that better? What good is it, being the Father of Science Fiction, if you can't brighten up your children now and then?"

No Place Like Home

I opened my mouth to thank him, but another voice erupted from the darkness.

"*Ç'est de conneries, mauvais Anglais!*" it barked. "*Qui est la père de la science-fiction?*"

My French was rusty, but I knew from this new interloper's tone that he objected strenuously to what Wells had just said: "The Father of Science Fiction." There were a few contenders for the title. But this stentorian Frenchman was not Hugo Gernsback, the Manhattan publisher. Nor was it Swift, of *Gulliver's Travels* fame—he was Anglo-Irish. Nor was it Edgar Allan Poe, thank God. And as for the writer whom I privately held to be the first true author of SF? Well, *she* was not French, either. There really was but one possibility.

"Monsieur Verne," I said, "please calm down. There is a sleeping child here."

The ghost of Jules Verne was thinner and more hirsute than his fellow phantom, but in attire they could well have been twins. I reflected that, even though Verne passed away some 40 years prior to Wells, he was clearly ahead of his time in sartorial matters—or else Wells' wardrobe was not as forward-thinking as his pen.

In any case, Verne made for a hot-headed cold case. Switching to English, the novelist continued his tirade. "Zis is an outrage! Why ze Powers send zis *connard* to do my job? Eee is no fit man to tcheer you up, wit' ees invisible mans and ees wars of de world!"

"Well, I'd very much like to hear your opinions too, Monsieur." I tried to be diplomatic, although between you and me, I had never been much of a fan of Verne's work, which I suspected lost something in translation.

But my mediation was in vain, for Wells cut me off. "I am precisely the man. This miserable writer—" he meant me, and I inferred that he meant *I felt miserable*, not—well, anyway—

Christmas Stalkings

"has already benefitted from my broad perspective on world events. The future—" He began at this point to retrace the floating graph.

Verne was having none of it. "Ze future was mine before it was yours! All zese things which I foresaw!"

"Yes," sneered Wells, "the twenty-first century has, indeed, borne out your prophecies. Hot-air balloon technology is booming."

"*Toujours avec le ballon!*" Verne spat. "What about ze gas-cab, or vat you call ze automobile, heh? Ze buildings which scrape ze sky? Ze picture-telegraph?"

I tried another olive branch. "I didn't know you predicted all those, Monsieur. Which books were they in?"

"It doesn't matter," sniffed Wells, returning to his graph work. "What the Frog here fails to realize is, I was sent here not to boast, but to boost. My later utopian writings—"

"Utopia!" Verne hollered, "You do not know ze meaning of ze word!"

"Indeed I do," huffed Wells, taking the bait. "It derives from the Greek. It means 'no-place.'"

"No-place is where *you* deserve to be!" spat Verne; then he bolstered this weak comeback by launching forward to disrupt Wells' graph. "Zis is ze trajectory of a true *optimiste!*" Verne began inscribing his own line through the air—a straight line as high as he could reach. He punctuated it with call-outs to his own utopian greatest hits. "*From ze Earf to ze Moon! Une ville flottante—Ze Floating City! Ze Mysterious Island! Ze Begum's Millions!*"

"Oh, jolly good," scoffed Wells. "You wrote the same thing five hundred times. Somebody pin a medal on this one."

"Gentlemen," I said, "this isn't helping. Can't we—?"

"There, you see? Our subject has dismissed you. He seeks practical solutions to the global issues that humanity has

No Place Like Home

wrought. Not penny-ante, pie-in-the-sky nonsense like your books disgorge."

"Zis, from ze man who tinks zat Martians with heat rays would invade ze Earth wizzout first getting zeir flu shots? *Ta geule!*"

"Real problems," Wells repeated. "Climate change. The lack of non-renewable resources. And...and something about the North Pole?"

"It doesn't matter —"

"Aha!"cried Verne. "Ze Norf Pole, you say? As in, perhaps, *Ze Purchase of Ze Norf Pole?* Published *dix-huit cent quatre-veignt neuf.* Eat zat, H.G.!"

"Yes, in which you predict, I believe, that a private gun club purchases the pole via auction, so they can fire a cannon at it to adjust the Earth's axis? What utter rubbish!"

"Well, it didn't work in ze book, but..."

Off they went. There was no interjecting, and if their quarrel kept growing in volume, they were liable to wake the toddler. How could I stop them, without betraying some preference for one or the other? They both wanted to be the Father of Science Fiction. Surely the genre was enlightened enough that it could handle having two daddies?

Yes, as I watched their bilingual argy-bargy, I realized their egos were eclipsing the real issue. They both seemed to genuinely want to help me, they just didn't quite know how. And there was my own dilemma, in stereo. Weren't we all, all three of us, nerdy writers, closet optimists, utopians searching for a mythical "no-place," eager to fix each other's problems, but clueless where to start?

I caught my reflection in the dark, flat screen. To show you how low I had sunk, I almost found myself preferring *Santa Claus Versus the Martians*. But that truly wretched thought sparked an idea. And that idea set me in motion.

⚞ *Christmas Stalkings* ⚟

Scott Sharplin

As I raced down the stairs, I drew no attention from the bickering ubergeeks — they were now embroiled in a match of sci-fi oneupsmanship unrivaled since the first Kirk vs. Picard Wars of the early Internet. I double-stepped down three flights, to the basement. Swiftly, I flipped breakers left and right, hoping against hope I'd remembered the right pattern.

Three flights up, I heard Wells bellow, "And who in bloody blue blazes would ever *want* to *Journey to the Centre of the Earth*?"

And then...the screaming stopped. I hurtled back up to the kitchen. Through the front windows, my Christmas lights flashed out a rainbow. Yes! Success! Yet for my plan to succeed, I was counting on the relative naiveté of two old ghosts whose eyes were fixed upon the universe.

"Oh no!" I cried. "The Martians are invading!"

I heard — "Good Lord!" "*Mon dieu!*" — so I knew I had their attention. I ran to the front door, threw it wide, then fairly leaped upon the lawn to execute Stage Two of my strange plan. It ran an awful risk of waking up the toddler — to say nothing of the neighbours, who'd be in their rights to have me straitjacketed and jailed. But it was the only way I knew to give the sad, bewildered ghosts their due.

"BEEP! BEEP! BEEP BEEP! BEEP BEEP!" I thumbed my car's alarm fob. "It's the Martians!" I called again. "That must be the sound of their...atomic...missile...gun! Run for your lives — if you have any!"

I looked up towards my own house. Above the holiday Morse code of the lights, I saw two glowing faces, phasing through the wall, their eyes raised up towards the stars. Beyond the beeping, I heard Verne's excited voice: "Ze missile gun! I had not taught of dat!"

"We must stop it, somehow," said Wells.

"But how? Anozer gun of ballistically similar proportions?"

"It's possible. Or germs!"

Christmas Stalkings

No Place Like Home

And with that, the brace of undead authors sprang out through the wall and bounded across the sky into the night. I smiled for them. They had a mission now, though ludicrous and vain. It kept them in motion, airborne like balloons, and a straight line is always better than a plunge.

"Boop." I fobbed the car alarm into silence. The blue-gray snow upon my lawn was painted with rainbows. My back still ached from hanging the lights, but in this quietude, it seemed worthwhile.

Then, from within: a long, low sob. The toddler was up after all. Another holiday tradition, I thought: lack of sleep.

I climbed up to the family room where he sat, weeping in confusion. I spoke soothing platitudes and stroked his hair until he calmed. I couldn't tell if he had seen the ghosts; he claimed not to have seen anyone, but then he asked me what I'd been talking about.

"Well, Papa had a visit from some...friends. And we were all trying to talk about the future. Which is tricky when you all have different presents."

"Oh." His eyes grew bright. "Can I have presents too?"

"Not for a couple more weeks, buddy."

"Okay." His mind returned to the fog of half-dreams. Finally he fished out one word from the night, and asked me, "What's a utopia?"

"Hmm." My reflex was to answer as Wells had, but then I thought of a quasi-literary, half-synonym for "no-place" that seemed right, after all. "It's home, bud. Utopia is home."

Christmas Stalkings

Scott Sharplin

Author Notes

Before writing "No Place Like Home" for the 2015 Gaudy Night, I participated in all the previous years' events, presenting an assortment of Robertson Davies' stories (my favourite is "Offer of Immortality"), and even writing one for 2014, the year we formally "crossed over" to completely original fiction. My inaugural tale featured the ghost of Clement Clarke Moore, as well as a demonic Santa Claus, and served to introduce the motif of fatherhood, which persists throughout both its sequels.

Unfortunately, when approached about this anthology, I found that story had vanished from my hard drive like an exorcised spirit. As my first stab at this rarefied genre, its absence need not be lamented, but its brief existence serves to explain why, in the preceding tale, my narrator reacts with such nonchalance when his Yuletide is disrupted by another ghostly guest.

Todd Pettigrew

Life Writing for the Lifeless

My friends, I must begin my remarks tonight with something of a confession. When I have spoken previously to you about my encounters with spirits, I may have left you with the impression that my first brushes with the supernatural have occurred only these past two years, coincident with this storytelling event. Indeed, since my fellow readers have likewise been visited by spectres recently, I am forced to wonder whether the very act of telling ghost stories functions as a kind of ethereal lightning rod. One publicly avows that one believes in ghosts, and the ghosts, for ghosts are always drawn to believers, come running.

Or, floating, as the case may be.

And while Pettigrew's Ectoplasmic Postulate may turn out to have paranormal merit, I must admit to you tonight that these past few years did not, in fact, mark my first encounters with ghosts. The events were so affecting, in fact, that for a time I tried to convince myself that they were the products of a fevered brain, too much overtaxed with study. But in my heart I knew what had happened, and I am now, at long last, ready to tell the tale.

It was December of 1993, and I was a graduate student at McMaster University in Hamilton, Ontario. One of my courses that year was with the distinguished literary biographer Jefferson Queene, who frequently gave a graduate seminar in what he called "Life Writing." Though some lesser students rather crudely called it "All Writers Turn Out to be Gay" behind his back.

Todd Pettigrew

The best thing about the class was that one could tailor it to one's own interest. If you were a fan of, say, Virginia Woolf, you might do a presentation on the great novelist's debt to her close friend Vita Sackville West. Or, say, Oscar Wilde and his extremely close friendship with Alfred Douglas—okay, fine, some of the writers did turn out to be gay, but that is in itself a perfectly legitimate thing to study, and in any case, you didn't have to select those authors if you didn't want.

You could choose Shakespeare, as I did.

And you would not necessarily have to focus on the beautiful young man to whom the Bard addressed 126 sonnets.

Besides, there is a very amusing story about Shakespeare seducing the female lover of Richard Burbage and renaming himself William the Conqueror in the process.

But these kind of rumours were hardly worthy of a young grad student with dreams of a professorship in some far off— and exotic—locale. Perhaps an island somewhere?

No, what I needed was a unique angle. Something that had never been considered before, but when it comes to Shakespeare, that is next to impossible.

And so it was that night, a few days before the end of term. In grad school, deadlines are fairly flexible, but it is universally understood that handing in something from the fall term after Christmas or, heaven forfend, in January, was a mark of shame upon a student that would never wash off. I simply had to finish. But I needed inspiration. A unique view of Shakespeare.

That was the year I coined the term "Scholar's Christmas." For while most people see their holidays as a chance to be freed from work, academics see the large blocks of unstructured time as a chance to get the things done that they hadn't had a chance to get done while classes were in session.

Life Writing for the Lifeless

A Scholar's Christmas, like a busman's holiday, is scarcely Christmas at all.

Seeking inspiration, I decided to work by candlelight. I thought perhaps the absence of modern illumination would somehow connect me to the figures of the English Renaissance that I so wanted to understand. Shakespeare primarily, but I also thought I could come to understand him through the lesser figures in his life. Anne Hathaway, the woman he supposedly was forced to marry when she became pregnant. His fellow writers, Marlowe and Jonson. Or, Beaumont and Fletcher, who, it was said, were involved in an ongoing, sexy three-way with their maid.

And so I worked, late into the night of December 23rd, reading everything I could get my hands on related to the English Renaissance, its authors, its history...until I fell asleep amid a pile of books.

Sometime later I awoke in a haze. A literal haze. One of my candles had fallen over and partially ignited a volume on Elizabethan dramatists, and though it was only the work of a minute to extinguish the flames, the room had mostly filled with acrid smoke, which left me choking and fanning the air trying to collect myself.

Just as I came to my senses, I saw the figure of a man. This, of course, was strange enough in itself, for who would be troubling with me on this bleak December night? I had nothing to steal — certainly no good ideas. But as the smoke began to dissipate, I noticed he was even stranger than I could have imagined. His clothes were dark and heavy, not at all modern, not even of this era. Instead of trousers he wore breeches, and a woolen doublet. His sleeves had the slashes characteristic of the sixteenth century and he wore a ruff about his neck. And as for his face, why, there was something familiar. The penetrating eyes, the thin beard, an air that only came from a life in the theatre. Could it be — ?

↳ *Christmas Stalkings* ↳

Todd Pettigrew

"Christopher Marlowe, at your service," said the figure.

"Rats!" I said.

"Rats?" he cried, somewhat alarmed.

"Oh, sorry," said I, my scholarly reflexes kicking in. "Of course you wouldn't like rats. Because they carry the plague."

"Rats carry the plague?" he screamed, looking about him even more wildly than before.

"Well, fleas, actually," I mumbled. "See, the fleas bite the rats... and oh, never mind." I found my way back to my chair.

We remained in the candlelight, silent for some time.

Finally the ghost—and here I reach the essence of my confession—broke the silence and spoke.

"What are these books over which you toil? The type is remarkably clear. The illustrations, so life-like. The printers of London could take some lessons."

"They are about you, actually."

"Me," he said brightly. "Then we have that in common." He winked. "We are both fascinated by the same thing."

"Well, not just you," I hastened to point out. "You and your contemporaries. And your world. And, of course, Shakespeare."

"Ah yes, they were grand times what with London teeming with every manner of— Wait, what do you mean, '*of course*, Shakespeare'?" His eyes narrowed with suspicion.

I felt suddenly anxious. How much does a ghost know of the intervening years between the end of his mortal life and his spiritual visitations to the world of the living? "Oh," I said, trying to sound breezy, "just that he is, ahem, so... well, famous."

"Shakespeare? Famous?"

"Pretty famous."

"Known to all those who read plays?"

"Oh yes."

"Regarded as a genius?"

"Universally."

"More famous than I?"

The candlelight flickered during another long pause.

"Say no more," he barked, turning away from me and looking out a window into the dark night. Then he turned his fierce eyes upon me once again. "You were hoping for him!" he declared.

"Him?"

"Just now, when I materialized, you had a look of hopeful anticipation that fell away when I announced myself. You were hoping I was Shakespeare!"

"Well, what if I was?" I said, in a raised voice. My usual pattern with ghosts is immediate fearful deference followed by misguided anger when the spirit begins to try my patience. "He is the greatest writer of an age, and when the walls of time and space fall away, I get stuck with the second banana."

That bit about the banana was deliberate. I knew he wouldn't get it and I thought that might put him in his place. It worked. Marlowe looked confused, then dejected, and then sat sadly in the seat across from me.

"I don't understand," he said confidentially. "My plays drew thousands to the theatres. My *Tamburlaine* was a revelation. My *Jew of Malta* was heralded as genius. My *Faustus*—" Here, he broke off in morose wonder. I felt bad for bringing him low in this way.

"All wonderful plays," I said. "And still frequently read by scholars and some still performed. It's just that they are now viewed as, well..."

"As what?" snarled Marlowe, the fire beginning to return to his eyes.

"As...preliminary," I said haltingly.

"Preliminary to what?"

"Well, you know..."

"To Shakespeare?"

"Yes. Your *Edward II* laid the groundwork for Shakespeare's historical masterpieces like *Richard III* and *Henry V*. Your *Faustus* for his high tragedies like *Othello* and *Macbeth*."

"Good heavens," he moaned. "How many masterpieces did he write?"

"Around forty, depending on what you count."

"So many. I wrote only half a dozen or so. But why..."

I remembered reading that ghosts sometimes have hazy memories of their own lives. Marlowe was struggling to recall the end of his.

"It's because you were murdered." I suppose that was a bit indelicate, but the hour had grown late.

"Murdered?"

"Yes, I was just reading about it. At a pub in Deptford. Stabbed in the eye."

"And Shakespeare?"

"Lived into his fifties. Retired a wealthy man. Said to have died after overdoing it at his daughter's wedding reception."

"And remembered as the greatest maker of plays in history," said Marlowe, disconsolate.

"Yup."

"Well, then," said Marlowe, a diabolical spark in his eye again, "let's see what he has to say for himself!"

He grabbed one of still-lit candles and plunged it into the nearest book. The volume leapt into flame in a way that ordinary science could not have accounted for—the blaze clearly aided by the supernatural quality of the candle-bearer.

The flames gave off dark, sooty clouds of smoke which billowed and swirled and began to coalesce into a shadowy figure. As before, it gradually took shape, and revealed the early modern details of figure, costume and stance, until the apparition said, "Ben Jonson, of the South Bank."

≥ Christmas Stalkings ≤

"Damn it," I said.

"Rats!" said Christopher Marlowe.

"Rats?" cried Ben Jonson in alarm.

"Apparently they carry the plague," said Marlowe.

"Good heavens!" said Jonson.

And thus began a good deal of *zoundses* and *gadzookses* and *merries* and many things denounced as foul and not worth a *groat*, until finally Marlowe returned us to order.

"Who is this man?" he asked. "He is not Will Shakespeare, I can tell you that."

"Another playwright," said I. "The other great contemporary of Shakespeare."

"More famous than I?" demanded Marlowe.

"Not really," I replied.

"Well, there's that."

"I beg your pardon," said Jonson, "but I was no man's contemporary. Other men were contemporary of me. I was the great poet and playwright of my era. Shakespeare was an unlearned scribe compared to me. Did you ever hear him attempt Latin? He kept confusing the nominative with the dative. The dative! To say nothing of his Greek. I, on the other hand, was conversant even in Hebrew!"

"Yes," I said, "but you yourself wrote that Shakespeare was not for an age, but for all time."

"Oh. That," said Jonson. "The man had died. I had to say something. But," he said, turning to look at his fellow ghost, "am I to understand that you are the great Christopher Marlowe?"

"Your servant," said Marlowe with an elegant bow.

"Ah, sir, it is an honour to meet you. I always admired the strength of your verse."

"You called it his 'mighty line'," I said, trying to be helpful.

Todd Pettigrew

"Don't interrupt, boy," said Marlowe, who, I hasten to point out, was not much older than I at the time. Unless you count the four hundred years he had been dead. Which, I guess you should.

What followed was, to paraphrase Shakespeare as I often do, long to tell and tedious to hear. It was mostly Jonson lavishly complimenting Marlowe on his plays and fishing for compliments of his own, which were hard to come by since Marlowe had been dead for years before Jonson made his debut. They bonded over many things — their hatred of creditors, their overbearing fathers (Marlowe's wanted him to be a cobbler like himself, ditto for Jonson, except with bricks instead of shoes), and their resentment of Shakespeare, who, it seemed, was not going to be making an appearance after all.

And then as the dawn grew nigh, a thought occurred to me, and, as Marlowe generously conceded that the Roman general Sejanus sounded like an excellent tragic hero and that Jonson's failure with his own Sejanus must have been Shakespeare's fault, for Shakespeare had acted a minor role in the play, I picked up my notebook and started writing.

For what was happening before me was infinitely more interesting than another paper about the life of Shakespeare. Here were lives that were shaped by the great man. Genius is, to some extent, inscrutable, incomprehensible, but the impacts of genius on the world and on those who inhabit it — in its joys and its griefs — never fails to fascinate.

We are all the heroes of our own life stories, but that is only one of the characters we play. We are also the supporting cast members in dozens of other life stories, and bit players in thousands more. In our story we are protagonists, the first person narrators, but what are we for others? The indispensable friend, the resentful ex-lover, last night's error of judgement, tomorrow's guardian angel.

Christmas Stalkings

These men, as much as any other of their day, pulled on the oars of their little boats, always in the wake of the great ship sailing beside them. I didn't want to know Shakespeare through them; I wanted to know them through Shakespeare.

And so it was that after another hour of this, I had the outline of a terrific paper that I was to call "Shakespeare's Other Lives: Marlowe, Jonson and the Shadow of Genius." And, as all academics know, the most important part of any paper is an impressive-sounding title. Once you have that, the rest of the essay more or less takes care of itself.

Thus, as the sun was about to rise on Christmas Eve, we all sensed that it was time for the spirits to depart. I was pretty sure Shakespeare said something about them having to do so in *Hamlet*, but I didn't think it appropriate to mention it just then. Jonson and Marlowe promised to keep in touch over the millennia and they thanked me for a pleasant evening.

As they were about to vanish, I felt I had to ask one more question. "Say, have either of you ever...you know...been... together...with a man...as one would with a woman?"

They paused and looked to each other blankly for a moment. And then Marlowe spoke "No idea what you're talking about." But he said it with a grin and he gave me a knowing wink as he faded from view. And so they were gone.

I returned, as I have for many years since, to my Scholar's Christmas, for I had a paper to finish.

Todd Pettigrew

Author Notes

Since Shakespeare has been the centre of so much of my life as a scholar and man of the theatre, it seemed sensible to do something with the ghost of the Bard. But I couldn't figure out what I would want the spirit of Shakespeare to say or how he would act. Consequently, I started toying with the idea of what Shakespeare's contemporaries might say if they returned to the world of the living. That led me to the dialogue about rats and everything else fell into place after that.

Jenn Tubrett

Bucky's Ghost

December 24th, 11:22 pm.
"Come on," Bucky whispered.

I marked his stop at the end of the wide dorm hallway by the stark white light of his cellphone flashlight. The three of us were the last students left on campus at Saint Anthony's Boarding School on the night before Christmas, so it was quiet—aside from the noise of the storm.

Never one to move easily in the dark, I held a candle that dripped wax onto my closed hand at every step. My cell phone battery had been down to its last bar long before the power went out. Rob had told me like eight times since the storm started to plug it in. Sage advice to be sure, but if you knew Rob as well as I did, you'd learn to brush off his constant warnings, too.

Rob was the young man to my left. Well, to my left and about three corridors back, tracing the tiles on the floor with the light cast from the screen of his phone, making sure he stayed between the cracks. He had a flashlight app as well, but claimed it was too bright and the well-polished floors sent it back to his well-cleaned glasses which meant he could go blind or something. I don't know. Like I said, it's Rob. You tune him out.

"Hurry up!" Bucky hissed, swivelling his light down each side of the intersecting hallway, likely looking for signs of Mrs. Cradway. She was the only faculty member who remained on campus with us over the break.

I huffed and turned back. Ignoring the unpleasant sting of the wax, I grabbed Rob's hand and dragged him along the hall at a regular human pace.

"Claire..." he protested, but his only resistance was the small stunted steps he took to stay inside the lines of the tiles.

Rob sometimes forgot to avoid cracks when he walked, sometimes he only flicked a light switch off once rather than his standard seven times, and sometimes he even went a full hour without washing his hands. But he was a little on edge tonight. We both were.

Before the power had gone out we were gathered in the small dining room, listening to Bucky's mostly-fabricated stories about the sordid history of this campus. Most of them involved this ghost he would show us tonight, his "Christmas ghost." But there were other ghost stories he liked to drag out when he had our full attention. Including, but not limited to, a collapse during construction of the East Wing. He'd told us three of the construction workers were killed in the wreckage and the reconstruction was built over their mangled corpses. Also there's the massacre he claims happened around the turn of the century. Pretty standard story: an overworked teacher breaks his sanity bone and cuts down fifty students in the Grand Hall before finishing himself off. Tonight he added the part about it happening on Christmas Eve.

"When the halls were near empty and a storm raged wild. Like tonight," he said, gasping dramatically as if he had just made the connection. "Just like tonight."

He also liked to claim that this place used to be a courthouse with a gallows out front and that the campus grounds were littered with the roaming ghosts of thieves, murders, and traitors. They form what he called the "Parade of the Guilty Dead" and scoop up unsuspecting students who get caught on the parade route.

Bucky's Ghost

Of course, all of these stories are total BS. Sure, there was a collapse during construction and three workers were injured; one of them spent the rest of his life in a wheel chair, but nobody died. I've heard about five different versions of the Grand Hall massacre story. How could a teacher gather fifty students on Christmas Eve when there's rarely more than half a dozen on campus? And a courthouse? Our campus was built on such a quiet edge of Cape Breton Island that most people didn't even know we were here. There's barely a street around this place and there has never been anything resembling a town, village, or city. If that all wasn't enough to convince me that Bucky was full of it, he'd also once told us that an old British librarian warned him that this school was built on the mouth of hell. Sound familiar?

As we approached, Bucky shone his light under his chin, illuminating his chubby face. "Zee ghost is zis vay," he said in a poor impersonation of Arnold Schwarzenegger — for reasons that made absolutely no sense in this context. We had watched Terminator 2 last night, so I expected to hear him butcher that accent at least until the New Year.

I sighed silently as I watched them. Rob, having found his rhythm, skipped from tile to tile to catch up with Bucky, now shining his light at the ceiling. *Merry Christmas, Claire. Enjoy your surrogate family*. Really, neither of them were that bad. Tonight was Christmas Eve and I was already having a better time than I did last year with my family. When my dad called yesterday to say he was stuck in Tokyo on business, I was actually relieved.

"There, there, there it is!" Bucky yelled.

"Shhhhhh!" Rob and I both said, probably matching him in volume.

I looked at the ceiling where Bucky's light hovered. There was a hatch that I had never noticed before. It ran about

Jenn Tubrett

fifteen feet long and three feet wide with a metal pull cord shining in the light.

"What is that?" I asked.

"The attic," Bucky said.

"The attic's in the East Wing."

"This is the old attic, before the extension. This is the only way in. It's blocked off from the new section. Safety reasons, I think. Floors are rotted out or something."

"Gee, I can't wait to go up there," I said.

"Claire," Rob protested, failing to detect my sarcasm, "there could be mold, or asbestos, or spiders, or—"

"A ghost?" Bucky asked, turning his light back to his face. "Well, do you want to see him or not?"

Rob and I exchanged a look. Yes, we did want to see him. I had first heard of the librarian's ghost almost two years ago. It was our eighth grade Spring Break and only Rob, Bucky, myself, and a handful of other kids were left on campus. I wanted to see it then, but Bucky said the ghost only comes on Christmas Eve. I always thought that was a convenient excuse, considering he was here alone that previous Christmas break and likely to be here alone for the next one. But I was wrong. Rob had been here with him for our ninth grade Christmas break.

Rob didn't see the ghost. He claims to have heard it and chickened out. His exact words were, "I heard it and I chickened out."

So now Rob was desperate to redeem himself, Bucky was desperate prove himself, and me? Well, come on! It's a ghost. Of course I wanna see a fricken ghost...or prove Bucky wrong. Either one and I would consider this a Merry Christmas all round. Also this: sneaking around after lights out and exploring during a black-out, made me feel...I don't know, older, I guess. Now that we were in Grade Ten, we were technically high school students, but it was the same ship-away boarding school, the same indifferent parents, the same grossly-enthusiastic teachers, and the same geeky friends. I wanted something to feel different. I wanted to feel more grown up and this little adventure seemed like something my childish middle school self would never have done.

"How are we supposed to get up there?"

Rob gasped. "Oh, Bucky, the ladder."

"Right, the ladder," Bucky said snapping his fingers. "Ya know, I had a feeling that I was forgetting something. Nagging at me, like it might have been something important."

I sighed and leaned against one of the many bookshelves that lined the wall. The dorm hallways were "quiet zones," filled with books and benches where students were encouraged to "sit, learn, and reflect." Really though, to "shut up and behave," at least that's how it always seemed to me. "Nah, it's just twenty-five feet up," I said, rolling my eyes.

"No, he's right, Claire," Rob said. "The ladder was important."

I rubbed my eyes. "Jesus."

"Gesundheit," Bucky said as he scanned the hallways with his cell phone. The light flitted over a poster for a fundraiser the student council organized before break. *Repair the water damage in the Grand Hall!!!* it read, with a series of overtly aggressive exclamation points. The caption underneath read: *Who wants to look up at the hundred foot ceiling of our glorious Grand Hall and see this?* Underneath, was a photo of the hideous brown water spot, perfectly centred in the white plaster ceiling. This is what was considered a cause worth fighting for around here.

"Claire, you're a genius," Bucky said when his light landed on me.

I shrugged. "Well, yeah, compared to you two, but, really boys, who—"

Jenn Tubrett

"No, the bookshelf. Pull it over, I'll climb up and open the hatch. There's a drop-down ladder inside."

I turned and held up my candle to look at the shelf. It was tall, stopping about three feet before the ceiling. There were only a few books on this one. A full set of encyclopedias — circa before the Internet — stood on the second shelf. The shelf below it had a selection of dictionaries, both of the English and French-English variety. There was also one hard-cover copy of Macbeth that some superstitious drama geek undoubtedly removed from the Shakespeare collection in the play house. I had to hand it to Bucky. It could work. And good for him, he almost got through the whole year without one single useful idea, and with seven days to spare. The kid was on a roll.

The shelf creaked as we slid it out from the wall, but it echoed more like a whimper than a scream, so we just shushed it uselessly and continued until it was lined up under the hatch. It really wasn't as heavy as it looked, or, now that it was away from the support of the wall, as sturdy. I pressed on the shelves and felt the slightest bit of give at the center. I wobbled it easily with the tips of my fingers, and gazed through the dark over at the dim outline of my chubby friend.

"Bucky, I don't think this is a good idea."

"It'll be fine. You two just hold either side to keep it steady."

"But I don't think it will support your weight."

"Ah!" Bucky took a step back and placed his hands on his hips. "Me-ow, Claire. Sure, I may be festively plump, but it's the holidays for crying out loud. Who doesn't pudge up a little at Christmas time?"

"Sound logic there, buddy, but it's not going to stop you from crashing through this shelf to an untimely death."

"Now who's being a drama-queen?"

Christmas Stalkings

Bucky's Ghost

"You Bucky, it's always been you. You're always the drama queen."

He sighed. "Fine, the lightest one will have to climb up."

We both looked at Rob. He was the tallest by a good six inches, but also the skinniest by a lot more than that. Bucky scanned him with his phone light. When the light passed his chin he threw his hands over his face. "Watch it, Bucky! My eyes!" Then he dropped his hands and looked at us both. "What?"

I raised a brow at him and looked at the shelf. He followed my stare to the top of it then scrambled for his puffer, taking two long draws.

I huffed. "I'll go." I held my candle out to Bucky. "Hold this."

He had it in his hand for a full second before he said "Ow!" and dropped it, still lit, to the floor, shaking his hand as if he'd put it through a torch flame. "Stupid wax."

Rob gasped and shot his foot out to stamp out the flame. His foot landed on the crack between two tiles. "Oh no. Oh, this is not good." He began flicking his cellphone off and on, counting quietly to himself.

"Oh, for God's sake you two! Would you just hold the damn shelf?"

"Fine, geez," Bucky said.

"Sorry, Claire," Rob said.

They moved into position on either side so I could climb up.

Other than one askew one clicking back into its proper position, the shelves didn't budge. I was on the second to last shelf, still with the support of the top against my hips, when I was able to reach out and snag the cord. I expected it to be jammed, since no one uses this section of the attic anymore, so I gave it a good yank.

Jenn Tubrett

It opened so easily that I lost my balance and slipped. Rob tried to catch me, but really only managed to punch me in the ribs as we both fell to the floor. Bucky, ignoring his post, rushed around to help us. I watched the bookshelf wobble and thought *this is how I'm going to die* as I hissed, "Bucky, the shelf!" Just in time, he turned back and steadied it enough to keep it from crushing all of us. As this happened, one of the books careened from the top shelf. I shot my arm over my face just before it hit and flung it to the floor.

I glanced over at it. Macbeth. Maybe those theater geeks were onto something.

Breathing heavily, I looked at Bucky. "There had better be a ghost up there or I'm going to kick you in the face."

"Be careful vat you vish for."

"Ya know, I might kick you in the face either way." I stood up and stretched my back. There was a pain in my ribs where Rob had tried to catch me and my elbow throbbed. I'd feel it in the morning, but for now I was fine. Poor Rob stared at the floor tiles he had been sprawled over, looking as appalled as if he had fallen into a litter box. "Shake it off, buddy," I said as I helped him up.

Rob only nodded, focussed because we were close now, and reached up to finish extending the drop-down ladder.

Bucky went first, I followed, and Rob came last. At the top, I glanced back where my candle had fallen and regretted leaving it there. It was just as well, I realized, since I left my matches back in my room anyway.

Once we were all inside the pitch black attic, Bucky bent to pull up the hatch. "What are you doing?" I asked.

"In case Mrs. Cradway makes her rounds, I don't want her to figure out we're up here."

"Oh yeah," I said, "and she definitely won't notice the shelf in the middle of the hallway."

"I think she might notice that, Claire." Rob said.

Christmas Stalkings

Bucky's Ghost

"Morons. I am surrounded by morons."

"I'm just saying, it's kinda hard to miss."

"Oh my God, Rob, I—"

"Shhh, shhh," Bucky said, as he pulled the hatch shut. "Listen." He turned his flashlight app back on and shone it into the attic.

The room was so large that I couldn't see the end. The floor was made of exposed beams and grey insulation. He kept the light level, so I didn't see the ceiling. The space was empty save a few stacked crates against the wall about fifteen feet away to our left and a few more, farther back to our right. A biting draft blew through. I shivered and zipped my sweater up to my chin.

I heard dripping. Was there a leak? No, it was a scratching. Not a scurry sort of scratch like a mouse or rat would make. It was a slow—*schiiit, schiiit, schiiit*—so rhythmic that it could only be intentional. I sucked in a breath and grabbed Rob's hand. He gasped and tried to jump away from me.

"Stay on the beams," I said, holding him in place.

"Oh God, this is so unsettling," he said. I'd like to think he meant the empty, unfinished attic, the cold horror-movie breeze, and the mystery scratching sound. But unfortunately, I knew he meant that staying on the beams was unsettling because he was essentially walking on the cracks.

The sound seemed to be coming from the crates. Bucky held his light up and I pushed my free hand into his as something round and white began to rise up from behind them.

"God, what is it?" I asked so quietly that neither of them could have heard.

The white figure began to come toward us. "Boooooo," it said.

Boo? I let my mind catch up with my eyes.

⟡ Christmas Stalkings ⟡

"Oh, Bucky!" I said, releasing his hand and whacking him in the stomach. "You little shit."

"What?" he asked.

"Booooo!" the "ghost" said again as it closed the distance between us. What I was looking at was clearly a man standing under a white sheet.

"Very funny," Rob said, finally grasping sarcasm.

"Who the hell is that?" I asked.

"It's the ghost," Bucky insisted.

The man was within reaching distance, and, to be perfectly honest, a grown man hanging out in the attic of a boarding

Bucky's Ghost

school hiding under a sheet was a whole different kind of scary. So on instinct, I shoved him away.

My hands pushed into nothing but cold. The sheet only pressed inward, hollow underneath. Suddenly, my hands were so cold that they hurt. I brought them to my mouth to stifle the scream that wanted to claw out of my throat.

"Sorry, sorry, I'm so sorry," a man with a prim voice said, from under the sheet. It shook and the sheet fell to the floor. "I told young master Buckingham that this was in poor taste."

Standing before us was a transparent man in a transparent tweed suit wearing little, transparent, round-rimmed glasses.

He was real. There was a ghost in the attic of our boarding school. A little cliché, yeah, but holy cool. This was amazing! He was looking at us and talking to us. Bucky was right twice in one day — a whole other sort of phenomenon.

Bucky laughed. "No, it was awesome! Haha, you two are such losers. Rob, I thought you were going to pass out when he came up from behind the crates."

"Bucky?" I asked, quietly because I couldn't find enough breath for full voice. "You set this up?"

"Yeah!" he boomed. "Ya burnt!"

I held my palms out in disbelief. Not that he set this up, or that he had been having actual conversations with a ghost — because he had told us that. We thought he was full of crap at the time, but he still told us. But I had to ask the question that anyone in this situation would want to know. "Why the hell would you ask a *ghost* to dress up like a ghost?"

"To scare you guys!"

"But the ghost is scary enough!"

"Precisely what I said." The ghost shook his head. "But I'm afraid the young man insisted on the scratching and the rising and the 'boo,' whatever that's supposed to bloody mean."

🍃 *Christmas Stalkings* 🍃

Jenn Tubrett

"And it worked," Bucky said. "Nicely played, Jeeves."

"Young master, for the last time, my name is Carleton Nigel Winchester the Third." The ghost said, prissily plucking at the cufflinks on his shirt sleeves.

"Nah," Bucky said. "Your name is Jeeves."

"I think he would know his own name," I whispered, still not recovered enough to find my full voice.

"Thank you, young master..." He trailed off, looking at me for the first time. "You, you're not a boy."

"I...um...I'm..." I stammered, holy crap, the ghost was talking to me. "No. No, I'm not a boy."

He took a small sharp breath that brought his shoulders up. "Young Buckingham," he said, and I detected a teacher in his sharp, checking tone. "Did you not promise to bring other students?"

"Claire is a student here."

"They let girls attend now?" He rolled his ghost eyes. "I'm just going to say it. I am glad that I died a hundred years ago. Between," he gestured to Bucky, "this young man's appalling manners, young ladies in slacks, and," he looked at Rob. "And this. What is this? Are you a girl too, or just an impossibly trim young man?"

Rob didn't respond. Actually Rob hadn't moved at all since the sheet fell off.

"Well?" the ghost asked tapping his leg impatiently. "Speak, young man."

Rob's lips opened, he drew in a breath and, after a few painful "eh, um, ah" sounds, he said, "Meep."

That was it. Just "meep."

"Good heavens, what has the world come to?" He ran his hand tightly along his jaw line. "Young Buckingham, please tell me the other students you brought have more to offer than a female and the boy who says only 'meep.'"

"Ah, this is all I brought."

⚜ Christmas Stalkings ⚜

Bucky's Ghost

The ghost huffed. "We agreed upon five more."

"They're all that's left on campus."

The ghost snorted. "Times have certainly changed indeed." He took another moment to study Rob and me, then studied Bucky. I saw his lip form a small snarl. "Well, I supposed you'll have to do."

"Do for what?" I asked. "Bucky, what the hell did you bring us here for?"

"Uh, to scare you. Tell her Jeeves."

The ghost huffed again. "Yes. The agreement between young Master Buckingham and myself was that he would produce five more students and in return I would scare them for him in," he rolled his eyes, "whatever fashion he saw fit. And yet, I see only half the amount of students and they seem to be fully scared so forgive me for feeling that I may have been the slightest bamboozled in this matter." He straightened out his tweed coat and shrugged. "Come along, you three, it's already nearly midnight and I haven't much time. You're not six like the last time, but I must make do, I suppose."

He brushed past me, heading back in the direction we'd come, and I felt the icy air of him wash over me.

"The last time?" Rob asked, catching my wrist as I attempted to follow as well.

The ghost stopped and turned back to us, forming a twitching half smile. "Why, the last time I worked in my beloved library." He said after a pause.

Rob and I followed, farther behind, because Rob was now tracing the floor beams with the light of his cell phone screen. I had an uneasy feeling, which should not come as a great surprise considering that we were following a ghost through an old attic during a stormy black-out.

"Where are we going?" I asked as we came to a turn.

Jenn Tubrett

He and Bucky were so far ahead that the ghost had to call back to me. I could barely see Bucky's phone light anymore. "Oh, just this way. It's quicker to get to the library if we loop around the Grand Hall."

As I stepped from beam to beam, pausing on each to wait for Rob to make his careful step, I felt a tingling in my mind, a sense of déjà vu. This was all very familiar. Not like Grandma's cookies, a favourite sweater, or well-worn pair of boots familiar. More like 'I should know better because...' But, I was too jittery — shaking with excitement, fear, and, most prominently, the cold — so my thoughts couldn't complete the loop.

"Come along, children. Catch up, catch up. It is most important that we all complete this last leg together."

"Six!" Rob gasped in an excited whisper. He clutched his hand over my forearm to stop me as they continued ahead. "Is this all starting to seem like one of Bucky's other horror stories?"

"Yes!" That was exactly it. I had heard something like this just earlier today, but I couldn't quite close my brain around it. "But I don't remember any dead librarians."

"The Grand Hall Massacre," he whispered.

I felt my face grow even colder as all the blood rushed out of it. "It was six, Claire. Bucky said fifty, Craig Wilson told me twenty-five, and Jeanne Crane said thirteen, but Mr. Howard told me that, in the only version around when he was a student here, it was always six.'

"Bucky!" I hollered and abandoned Rob to run after him. Damn idiot! He told us the damn story! How did he not piece this together? Sure, I was still missing some pieces, and I had no idea how a ghost could kill a living being, short of scaring them out a window or...down a hole. Wait! The water damage! In the ceiling of the Grand Hall! This creep was trying to send us all falling to our death!

Christmas Stalkings

Bucky's Ghost

"Bucky!" Rob now ran next to me, his light waving with the motion of his arm. My guess was that he had come to the same conclusion that I had. Inability to detect sarcasm aside, Rob was a pretty bright guy. "Bucky, stop!"

We made it around the turn and I breathed a breath of relief to see Bucky standing there. The ghost was twenty feet beyond him. "Chill, guys," Bucky said. "Jeeves told me to wait for you."

The ghost took one look at our panicked faces and snarled. "Now, young master, hurry!"

"Bucky!" I shouted, as he obediently moved forward.

"Come on!" he said cheerfully, gesturing for us to follow, and began to trot toward the ghost.

"No!" Rob and I both shouted as the beams cracked under Bucky's feet.

I didn't stop to think. Had I done that, this story might have ended very differently for poor stupid Bucky. But I didn't. I leapt onto the beam flanking the one Bucky stood on and hooked my arms under his. He let out an anguished yelp as the beam under him gave way and I yanked him toward me. His weight brought me down hard. I landed on my bottom and the beam that took the impact released a terrifying creak. I almost lost my hold on Bucky as he sank into the brand new hole in our Grand Hall ceiling. I managed to lock my hands around his chest even though my arms felt as if they were being torn from my body. Then the beam under me snapped like a bone breaking and I saw splinters fly. The beam sunk, and we both screamed as it dropped us what felt like eight feet, but was probably only inches.

Out of the corner of my left eye, I saw Rob fall. For one awful moment I thought he was going down too, but he reached out and grabbed Bucky's arm. We both pulled him back out of the hole and scrambled in a tangle of limbs, like a beached octopus, to the next beam.

Christmas Stalkings

Jenn Tubrett

"No! No! NO!" the ghost shouted from across the chasm Bucky had created.

"Jesus. Jesus. Jesus." Bucky said as he gasped for air.

Rob and I didn't allow time for him to recover. Without so much as exchanging a look, we each grabbed one of his arms and towed him along with us as we ran.

"No!" the ghost shouted again, as he dropped to his knees and slammed his fists down. The entire attic shook as we hurried back the way we had come. The first five or six beams we went over collapsed as we cleared them and the rest continued to crack.

"You come back here, children! You come back here and die!" commanded the livid-faced spirit of the professor.

"Yeah, no thanks!" I shouted.

He ran after us, his every movement pulsing through the attic like an electric shock.

I overshot a beam and the back of my heel scraped painfully over it as I lost balance. I barely even felt the surface beneath me before Rob's long arms shot under mine. He set me back on my feet. We made the last turn and were almost back to the hatch.

"You will die," the ghost said, no longer shouting. That was even more frightening than his outrage. "You will die just like the others. I will see —"

And then it stopped. The voice, the pulsing, the cracking boards.

We weren't stupid enough to let that slow us down. Well, Bucky stopped to look back, but I shoved him forward. "Go, go, move!"

The hatch opened easily. I sighed with relief at the open hallway and the bookshelf that stood misplaced at the centre. We climbed out.

Then we stood stunned in the hallway. I coughed up dust and picked at the wood splinters in my sweater. Bucky shone

Bucky's Ghost

his light up through the hatch and I squeezed Rob's arm, fully expecting the ghost to be there for a horror-movie style, pop-up, final scare. Nothing happened.

"Where did he go?" Bucky asked, turning his light on me.

I looked at his cellphone. "It's midnight," I said with relief. "Jesus Bucky, do you remember anything about the stories you tell us? He only comes on Christmas Eve. His time his up."

Rob chuckled a disbelieving laugh. "It's a Christmas miracle."

Bucky put a hand on each of our shoulders. "God bless us, every one."

"You're an idiot," I said, swatting his hand away.

"Well, I wasn't wrong about the ghost, was I, Claire?"

"Yeah, but maybe you could have had a bit more foresight about the murder."

"How was I supposed to know?"

I waved my hands out toward him. "It was your damn story!"

"I didn't have all the details, Claire. I didn't know it was only six kids and Jeeves said he was a librarian."

"Still!" I yelled. "The Grand Hall? Christmas Eve? It took Rob and me two minutes to figure it out!"

He placed his hands on his hips and posed primly. "Well, sooooor-ry we can't all be B-students like you and Rob."

"Actually," Rob said, tipping forward, "my average is A minus."

I chuckled weakly and shook my head, as exhaustion set in. "Come on, let's put this back together."

The boys held the shelf while I climbed up again to right the hatch. Once I hopped off, we pushed the shelf against the wall. I placed the copy of MacBeth back from where it had fallen and scooped my candle up from the floor. We all took a moment to look around.

☙ *Christmas Stalkings* ❧

"How does it look?" Rob asked.

"Better than the Grand Hall, that's for damn sure."

"I assume, Claire, that the Grand Hall has a Bucky-sized hole in the ceiling."

I huffed. "Rob, I meant— Oh, never mind."

"What about him?" Bucky asked, looking up.

I shrugged. "Well, he's gone, for a year at least."

"What about next year?" Rob asked.

I sighed, slipped each of my hands into one of theirs and started moving us through the hallway toward our rooms. "We'll deal with that next year. And guys?"

"Yeah, Claire?" they both asked.

"Merry Christmas."

Author Notes

I have always identified as a horror writer. While I enjoy dabbling in a variety of genres, I always felt that my strongest voice was also my most frightening. So, when Ken asked me to take part in the most recent instalment of the annual Gaudy Night: Evening of Christmas Ghost Stories, I was thrilled. Having never attended one of these events before and being only moderately familiar with Robertson Davies, I purchased a copy of *High Spirits* from the Google Playstore. I read a few of his stories and then attempted to emulate him both stylistically and thematically.

It did not go well.

Bucky's Ghost

It seemed that whatever I wrote was either so obvious that it was boring or so exaggerated that it felt more like parody than imitation. The result was a series of partially written stories that were not only unrepresentative of Davies' work, but also had very little few similarities to my own. In the end (the end of the beginning, anyway) I decided to scrap the stories that I started and simply write my own interpretation of a Christmas Ghost story.

Bucky's Ghost was originally supposed to focus on the ghost. I chose to set it on a campus where my ghost had been an educator. To help keep it light and humorous, I wanted my other characters to be young teenagers, so I made it the campus of a boarding school. My original vision was of the students discovering and forming a relationship with this uptight, amusing, and fascinating ghost before discovering who he was. However, when I found myself more than half way through and the ghost had yet to make an appearance, I realized that the story was about the students and how they interacted with each other during this supernatural experience.

Because this was meant for a listening audience, it's meant to feel like it could be told around a campfire, not unlike the stories that Bucky tells to Claire and Rob. I knew it would be slightly off theme, but my goal was to capture a "classic" ghost story as it would seem to someone who grew up in my generation. I used a few references from my youth (although, The Terminator and Buffy are still totally relevant...right?) and some stock horror elements, like the ghost in the attic and the power outage, in an attempt to accomplish that.

The story was a pleasure to write and a joy to perform. I've made a few adjustments with the help of our editors to make my story more considerate of a reading audience. I only hope that the reader has as much fun as I did.

Todd Pettigrew

Ken's Tale

Ladies and gentleman, I know that a great many of you came here tonight with the expectation that you would be hearing from the redoubtable Ken Chisholm. It is my sad duty to tell you that Ken could not be with us tonight, but he did send a rather detailed email just a few moments ago explaining his absence, and with your kind indulgence, I would like to share it with you now.

Dear Todd,

I am afraid I will not be able to join you tonight for the annual event at the library. The story is a bit involved, but I thought that you deserved the truth. Please do not share this message with anyone else.

I was just beginning to set down the harrowing tale of a visitation by two lively spirits, one the ghost of Lewis Carroll, the other of a little girl called Carol Lewis. She claimed to be the original Alice in Wonderland, and that the story really ought to have been called *Carol in Crazyvania*. It promised to be a most enchanting yarn.

But sadly, writing is hungry work for me, and shortly after setting hand to laptop, I was filled with a desire for a sandwich. I had some turkey left over from Thanksgiving and rather thought that I should finish it off before it went bad. Moreover, the coming of the Yuletide reminded me that one of my gifts from last year, a real deli meat slicer given to me by my sister, was still in the box. The two things suggested a sliced turkey sandwich and so off I went.

Todd Pettigrew

It seems mad in retrospect, but eager to return to my writing as quickly as possible, it occurred to me that I could expedite my snack by preparing the bread and mayonnaise by hand at the counter while simultaneously slicing the turkey with my feet. Those who know me are aware of the remarkable dexterity of my lower limbs, particularly when I have removed my socks, but as I say, I have come to regret this culinary hubris.

At the risk of slowing down my tale, and now realizing that you, a noted ham, are likely to ignore my wishes that this missive not be shared, please do extend this warning to those assembled: never try to slice meat with your bare feet. The deli slicer is an effective device but it has no powers of discernment whatsoever. As far at the slicer is concerned, the human foot *is* a piece of meat and it will have no qualms at all about dashing off several ounces of your big toe, cut so tender and thin you could almost see through it. This is a quality admired in pastrami, but not in one's digit.

Todd, I confess to you here that, indeed, one of my little piggies went to market.

The rest of me went to the emergency room — once an open one was located — and after a rather embarrassing series of explanations (oh, why didn't I just say the cat did it?) I was treated first for a bleeding toe, and then for an infection which had set in at record speed, for apparently the turkey, which seemed quite fine to me, was "as rancid as a ten-dollar gigolo." These were the exact words of the attending physician.

Still, I returned home this morning, determined to finish writing down my tale of Lewis and Carol. My body and mind throbbed with pain, however, and my brain was so fogged by this agony, that I could not clearly read the label on the little bottle of painkillers I had been given. Uncertain, I decided to take the entire bottle at once, on the assumption that the pills would dissolve in my stomach gradually, one at a time.

Here you may give another warning to those assembled: pills taken *en masse* do not dissolve gradually in your stomach, one at a time. All those little devils dive right into your bloodstream simultaneously and they send you into a fevered sleep when you're trying to write a very serious story about Carol Lewis on your laptop.

When I awoke, I found myself face-to-face with yet another spectre. This one, stranger than any I had seen or heard of before. He was a man of indeterminate age, indeed, of indeterminate everything. His face seemed to change its features even as I gazed at it. So, too, did all his characteristics. At times he seemed tall, then short, then minuscule. One moment his hands were empty, the next he seemed to hold a book. His whole being resembled nothing so much as a character on an old TV where the channel was not properly tuned, which faded into and out of view with occasional images from another station appearing – images we used to call, I now remember, *ghosts*.

I asked the figure who he was and he immediately began to wail.

"I know not who I am! This is my curse, foolish man! I know only my name, no other details of my life."

I was about to ask his name, when something from his brief oration struck me.

"What do you mean, 'foolish man'?" I asked indignantly. "I'll have you know I am in some circles regarded rather as an intellectual. Why, this very night I will be appearing at the McConnell Library with two very distinguished members of the university faculty."

If it is possible for a ghost to blanch, white and faded as they typically are, well, I tell you this ghost did indeed go pale.

Todd Pettigrew

"Wait. McConnell, did you say?"

"Yes, and the men I am reading with are also very handsome and well-dressed," I said, though I don't know why.

"But that's my name!" the spirit shouted.

"Good Lord," I said, and then realized that this crafty phantom was changing the subject again. "Why 'foolish man'?" I insisted.

"Oh for God's sake, you've taken a whole bottle of medicine after nearly cutting your foot off making a sandwich," McConnell sneered. "The slicer is still on the floor covered in drumstick and a not inconsiderable amount of your blood. If you weren't so close to shuffling off the mortal coil even now, you wouldn't even be able to see me. Now tell me of this library."

"Well, as it happens, it is the McConnell Memorial Library. Perhaps it is named after you."

"It must be. The fates have brought me to you for this very purpose. I take it all back. You are just the man whose brain holds the answers that I have been seeking, lo, these many years. Tell me, who is this man McConnell after whom this great edifice of community learning is christened?"

"I have no idea," I replied.

"What?" shouted the ghost, his changes in appearance seeming to quicken. In one, I thought I made out the shadow of a firearm.

"It's just the name. I guess it's ironic when you think of it."

"Ironic?"

"Well sure. We always call things the So and So *Memorial* This and That, but then we don't actually *remember* who the person was. It's just the name of the thing. I mean, who is the Lincoln Monument named for?"

"For Abraham Lincoln, obviously!"

Ken's Tale

"Okay, that was a bad example. Who was Mt. Rushmore named for?"

"American businessman, Charles E. Rushmore; it had previously been known as Slaughterhouse Rock."

"How do you know all that, when you don't know anything about yourself?"

"I told you. It's a curse. Now please, is there no way you can find out anything about my history?"

"Oh, wait," I said, "I have my laptop right here. I'll bet the library site has a whole thing about you. Hold on...huh."

"What is it?" he asked impatiently.

"I don't actually see anything on the library site about the person it's named after. But don't worry, I'll Google it. How many McConnells could there be?"

It turned out there were quite a few.

First up was James V. McConnell, a celebrated marine biologist. "Do you feel like you might have been a celebrated marine biologist?" I asked the ghost.

"Maybe. I quite like seahorses."

"Wait. How is your hearing?"

"Fine."

"Not you then. This guy lost his hearing after being a target of the Unabomber, Ted Kacinski."

The spirit looked disappointed.

"Do you think you might have been pastor of the Whitewell Metropolitan Tabernacle?"

"Doesn't ring a bell."

"Doesn't matter anyway. He's still alive."

And so it went for hours, searching and searching for the needle James McConnell in a haystack of James McConnells.

There was James McConnell, the psychic; James McConell, the American professor of Spanish. A scientist in Guam, a dentist in Indiana, and a British composer who owns the domain name, jamesmconel.com.

Todd Pettigrew

"It's no use," I cried at last. "We'll never find the right James McConnell."

"Well, you did your...wait did you say *James* McConnell."

"Yes, I replied; it's the James McConnell Memorial Library."

"But my name is Richard McConnell!"

We both stood there in shocked silence for a moment and then he began to fade away. Whether it was because the pain killers in my system were finally wearing off, or that he had tired of me, or that he was being called back to whatever spectral realm he had escaped from, I shall never truly know.

But as he disappeared, I distinctly heard him call out, "You foolish maaaaaan!"

And so you see, Todd, there is simply no time left for me to relate a tale of ghosts despite my very best efforts.

Perhaps next year.

Your friend,
Ken

Author Notes

For a while I had entertained the idea of somehow using the ghost of James McConnell, after whom the library in Sydney is named, in a story. But I couldn't find out anything about him and so had no basis for a tale. But when Ken Chisholm had to cancel his appearance one year, and we needed a quick story to fill up some time, I thought it might be amusing to watch a silly, unrealistic version of Ken struggle with the problem rather than struggling with it

Christmas Stalkings

Ken's Tale

myself. Ken really did have an issue with his foot, though I may have taken some license as to how that difficulty arose.

Scott Sharplin

The Great Geisel

Permit me to begin this story with a quotation about stories. I know it runs the risk of laying the brickwork for one of those Moebius-loop narratives, the kind where pillows examine their dreamers, navels gaze back at their owners, and mirrors do that thing they do whenever they're hanging out in groups of three or four, and they have a few drinks in them and someone brings up M.C. Escher. But bear with me.

The quote comes from Sir Terry Pratchett, a talented, prolific Brit whose ghost I should be delighted to receive on this or any Gaudy Night—but who, having passed only this year into the Discworld in the sky, is likely still deluged with fans' requests for hauntings, visitations, or a cameo groan in the yuletide séance. And he'd probably prefer to spend his first Hereafter holiday season with dead family and friends— for, though Sir Terry was an avid atheist, he celebrated Christmas, at least in its modern, non-denominational form.

The quote! Forgive me. Thus: "There's always a story. It's all stories, really. The sun coming up every day is a story. Everything's got a story in it. Change the story, change the world."

As a semi-professional storyteller, I find this thought semi-inspiring. On the one hand, it makes my stock in trade more precious than diamonds—for if everything is a story, then we all need stories just to survive. But on the other hand, flood the market and demand will plummet. If stories are ubiquitous, then storytellers are extraneous. If the sun coming

Scott Sharplin

up every day is a story, then one hardly needs a bard outside one's window to extol its solar virtues.

At the very least, this quote has helped me understand why the Yuletide season is so commonly associated with the spinning of tales. "The sun came up," might be a story, but it's an old one; we've all heard it, three hundred and sixty-five times a year. But when the days grow short, the story gets suspenseful — till finally, we reach the Solstice, the longest night. A nail-biter. "Once upon a time, the sun...wait for it...*wait for it...*"

Here's another droll thing about stories. Even as a storyteller, I find them a great deal easier to *talk about* than to simply *tell*. Case in point: here I am, dragging my feet through a slushy, self-reflective prologue. You came for a tale of phantom wanderings, not my stale and random ponderings.

Yet, my story must commence at the same shameful point: my inability to tell a story. The night in question, three weeks past, was typical in that respect. I had an audience of one, impatient in his need for some soporific tale to aid his busy brain in winding down after a day of games, crafts, tantrums, mandatory mealtimes, and the thousand natural shocks that four-year-olds are heir to. Like most nights, the dialogue went thus:

"Papa, tell me a stowy."

"I already read you two chapters of *Le Petit Prince*, and a chapter of *The Secret World of Og*."

"I want one of *your* stowies."

"It's time to sleep, buddy."

"What are you going to do?"

"I—I have to send an email."

"And then what happens?"

"Then maybe...have a visitor. We'll see."

"And then what happens?"

The Great Geisel

"Then, I'll—Wait. You tricked me. This is not a story. Sleep."

"Is it Chwistmas yet?"

"It's not even December, dude."

"Have you decided what I get for Chwistmas yet?" This question, posed nightly since approximately Easter, was the drawback of raising a child free from the shackles of the Santa Claus myth.

And it was also a touchy subject for me, on this night in particular. "Please sleep."

"Will you tell me a Chwistmas stowy?"

"I don't know any Christmas stories."

"But—"

"Once upon a time, the sun came up. The end." If it was good enough for Sir Terry, I figured, it's good enough for the boy.

"I can't sweep. I'm scared."

"Dude, you're not scared." This was a tactic he'd obtained from some book or show or friend, and I knew it was a ruse. "Now, close your eyes, and count the sheep that sneak in underneath your eyelids. I'll be right next door. Sweet dreams." I made my escape before any more objections could be raised.

It was chill black beyond the windows, and most of the lights were off inside the house. I trod lightly to my office, where I hastily composed the aforementioned e-missive. "Dear Chris, Apologies for the delay. I would be happy to contribute another story to this year's Gaudy Night event. Although I have not, as yet, been visited by any authorial spooks, I'm confident that one will swoop down to inspire me as soon as I hit 'Send.' Gaudily Yours, Scott."

Click. The zeroes and ones winged their way through the ether. I paused then, heavy with the twin weights of anticipation and responsibility. When at last the pause began

Scott Sharplin

to feel awkward, I folded shut my laptop — plunging my surroundings utterly into the dark — and started speaking, swiftly yet softly, so as not to interrupt the sheep-count in the room next door.

"Okay, ghosts, confession time. I need a haunting, *stat*, and not just for the sake of Gaudy Night. In fact, I only said yes to Chris because agreeing to Gaudy Night seems to guarantee I'll wind up with some irritated spectre in my living room. But I need wisdom, and I think it's the sort that only comes through long life — or afterlife."

My feeble medium routine continued for a spell, and while I'll happily recount the highlights in a moment...first, I need to seize on the prerogative set by my story-conscious prologue, and interrupt myself to comment on my own narrative. This is not a critique — I'm not so self-deprecating as to slam my own story before it's even left the nest. In any case, compared to "Once upon a time, the sun came up," I rather think I'm nailing it. So, not a critique — a trigger warning, as the Internet would say. This is where things get...political.

"Yo, ghosts? I know you're not accustomed to coming on command, but some of you have proven eager to make house calls, so...shiver me timbers. Put me on your chain gang. I have to make a tough decision, and you seem to like popping up whenever I'm stuck, so...throw me a groan, here. No?

"It's about the refugees. I'm sure you've heard about them, even if you died pre-Twitter. Thing is, my wife and I...we want to help, we're looking to sponsor a family. And I know it's the right thing to do, but with our bank account the way it is...well, Christmas is expensive. And after looking at the numbers, I see it's going to come down to either one family or the other. And my son...this is the first year he really *gets* Christmas, and I'd hate to take all that away from him for some altruistic fancy. I need you to teach me! How can I pinch all his presents away without being a...Scrooge?"

Only silence answered me, and not even a promisingly eerie silence, either. I was grasping at trees and barking up straws. I got more specific.

"Might there be any Buddhist authors listening? Is Basho bashing around up there? Or rather...Herman Hesse, I guess? Could you unattach yourself from the unknown and come teach me a thing or two about letting go? Preferably in terms a four-year-old would understand.

"No takers? No, Buddhist authors don't become ghosts. They reincarnate—into editors, if they've been good, or critics, if they're rotten. But I clearly can't call on the usual clutch of Christian conjurations. They'd guilt me back into stuffing the stockings. But who, oh, who among the lifeless literati, would not jump to call a gift-less papa naughty? I have to find someone to give me an inch, or my son's sad expression will brand me a...killjoy.

"I have it! A humanist, wiccan, or pagan! Some atheist author who sees the big picture. Louisa May Alcott? Ralph Waldo Emerson? Margaret Laurence? Herbert Melville? Kurt Vonnegut? No, no, not Vonnegut; he's too contrarian. My kingdom for an undead Unitarian!"

I broke off here, as the absurdness of my desperation felt more palpable than even the darkness. I wanted to help some family I'd never even met, some abstract blur of victimhood, but I dreaded upsetting my own flesh and blood in the process. I envisioned an ironic sequel to my anti-Christmas story, wherein my disappointed son eventually grew up, embittered and cruel, to wreak his present-less vengeance on the world.

"Oh!" That thought made me think of one final option. "Oh! Yes, oh! O. Henry? Story Magi? D'you have a gift that could help steer me clear of this ironic twist?"

⚘ *Christmas Stalkings* ⚘

But O. was silent, like the rest of them. Perhaps he'd cancelled his service to the mortal world to buy some trinket for a lover, while his ghostly partner sold her own most precious thing to buy him an inter-planar iPhone. Or perhaps my dilemma just wasn't worth picking up for.

"I give up!" I lamented, more loudly than was needed. "There's clearly no story that won't leave him cheated. To help those in need, I must pilfer and pinch, till my son thinks his father's a rotten old..."

Wait. An idea. An awful idea. A wonderful, wonderful, awful idea.

I opened my mouth to invoke one last ghost. But before I could speak, the son came up—or at least, his voice did, from the bedroom next door.

"Papa? I *need* you to tell me a stowy!"

I ignored his pleas. He'd settle down, and besides, this was all for his benefit. To the darkness, I spoke: "Dr. Geisel? Hello? Dr. Theodor Geisel? It's one of your most avid writer-disciples. Should I call you Theo? Or—no, silly goose—it's clear you'd prefer to be called Dr.—"

"PAPA!"

"Keep counting sheep!"

"I need a Cwistmas stowy!"

"In a minute!"

Something was stirring in the umbral silence. I dearly hoped my ghost was on his way. And yet, a minute passed, and then another, and I realized I couldn't afford to wait for this spook to take the scenic route. If I didn't assuage the boy soon with some sort of story, he'd burst out of his bedroom. And if the spirit arrived *then*, there'd be a lot of awkward explaining to do. Not least of which was why I kept insisting that Santa Claus *wasn't* real, then went off and had lengthy chats with ghosts.

Where *was* he? I racked my brain, trying to recall what I'd

The Great Geisel

done in the past to summon spectres. Sickeningly, I realized they *never* came when called — only when it was convenient for them, and inconvenient for me. And usually when they had some sort of bone to pick — if that expression isn't disrespectful to the dead.

But maybe that's the ticket, I thought. Dr. Geisel wasn't going to come when called, but maybe — perhaps — he would visit if *galled*. Thinking quickly, I did what I knew would get under the skin of any self-respecting author — even those with no skin left.

"Well, I'll be Grinched if that Grinching grouch hasn't gone and Grinched me in the lurch. He's Grinchier than his creation. I would not Grinch him in a box. I would not Grinch him with a fox. I would not — "

"What in the name of the Lorax?" came a surprisingly gruff voice.

"Why the peace of the innocent do you disturb?
Don't you know the word 'Grinch' isn't meant as a verb?"

"Dr. Geisel!" I cried in relief. "And/or Seuss!"
"Both and either!" he boomed. "Now prepare your caboose.
For grammatical slights of this sort are, I find,
Swiftly fixed with a boot to one's errant behind."

"*Mea culpa.* But wait. First, I need your direction.
And then I'll accept my gluteal correction.
Instruct me, Sir Seuss, how I might cancel Christmas
Without my son thinking his father malic...mas?"

And here, as the ghost frowned a frown barely visible,
I feared he'd prejudged my intentions as risible,
So I rushed to explain: "When the Syrians come,
They'll have nothing — no cake — not so much as a crumb.
And I'd give all we have to help strangers in need,
If some story could help stem a toddler's greed."

Christmas Stalkings

Scott Sharplin

Now the stately pseudonymous author was nodding.
(I strained to refrain prematurely applauding.)
"I taste your dilemma — it's downright delicious —
To bring up a four-year-old non-avaricious.
But why not just read from the volume you pinched
When you summoned me here?
Why not read him *The Grinch*?
"'Maybe Christmas —'" And here his own volume he quoted
"'Doesn't come from a store'" — fresh as if he'd just wrote it.
"A classic," I said, "but it makes the Grinch *me*,
To have stolen the presents, the feast, and the tree.
I was hoping for something more flattering. Please —
Do you know any stories about refugees?"

Then the ghost up and laughed, like the problem was done.
"You're forgetting my roots. I'm American, son.
My grandparents were immigrants — German, in truth.
And I heard all their harrowing tales in my youth.
Of the needs of the needy, their flights out of fear
To a place where all refugees have cause to cheer.
Oh, such tales I can tell you. Such places we'll go!"
(And the phantom here practically started to glow.)
"We'll regale your young son with some yarns of largesse,
And true liberal benevolence, nobleness — yes,
Even martyrdom! He'll be stuffed full of such grace,
He'll surrender his toys with a smile on his face!"

"That sounds great —" I began, but the Doc was obliv'us,
Consumed by his cause like the uber-religious.

"It's what I believe in! It's all I have touted!
No evacuee should be outed or routed.
But greeted with love, be they Muslim or Jew.
We should all ask ourselves, 'What Would Dr. Seuss Do?'
As my stories reveal, I've respect for all chaps —

Christmas Stalkings

I'll receive them with love...well, except for the Japs."

"Wait, *what?*"
So caught up I'd become in his jingoistic rhythms, I'd nearly bobbed my head in agreement with even that offensive rhyme. The whole time, I thought Dr. Geisel had been spoon-feeding me green eggs and ham, but it now felt as though I'd swallowed a gut full of oobleck.

"What on earth," I sputtered, "could the writer of *Yertle the Turtle* possibly have against the Japanese?"

Seuss insouciantly shrugged. "It's not P.C., I know,
But if we want to win, then those Japs have to go.
For if not, with their hatchets our heads will be cleft.
We can get palsy-walsy with those who are left."

I still stood aghast. "Did you just compose a racist manifesto in anapestic tetrameter? I refuse to believe that the most beloved children's author this side of Lewis Carroll was a xenophobe."

"Look it up," chuckled Seuss. "And then, while you're online,
Look up Carroll as well—you won't like what you find.
Now, let's visit this boy of yours, spin him a fable.
I'll shy from that subject as much as I'm able."

"Thank you, but no," I said, in a deliberately arrhythmic phrasing designed to indicate that his galloping verses were no longer welcome here.

"Suit yourself. But good luck with the lad Christmas Day,
When you've nothing to give him, and nothing to say."

With that, the bigoted bugbear dissolved—or so I assume. I didn't bother to look, but instead propelled myself out of my chair and across the hall towards my son's room. The boy had been calling for me all this time, claiming to be scared and demanding stories, and I realized, with all the whiplash of the truly self-absorbed, that I was traumatizing him even

Scott Sharplin

now, as I sought out recourse for his future traumas. Perhaps the ghost of O. Henry was nearby after all.

The room felt Spartan in the dark, as if the gifts from all three yuletides past had been purloined. I sat on the side of his bed and murmured reassurances.

"I need a stowy," he insisted, the pint-sized mind-reader.

"Yeah, I know," I said. "A Christmas story. Lie down, dude. I'll do my best."

> It was long, long ago, in the East — near the Middle
> Where heat gets so hot that your heart starts to sizzle
> Though it might well have been near the end of
>   December
> But probably not — well, but who can remember?
> The Galilee ex-pats were all rearranging
> Because of a census — it's not worth explaining
> The point is, one couple had brought extra luggage
> A womb full of baby that made the mom sluggish
> But her fiancé helped in transporting the laddie
> (A modern relationship — more than one daddy)
> To Bethlehem, where from the signs they concluded
> No vacancy — save for one — livestock included.
> They weren't refugees, though their lives were as
>   cruel-la
> With camels for midwives, a dog for a doula
> But somehow, they managed. Push, breathe. The old
>   song.
> Yet another of God's many sons came along.
> And then, something with shepherds? An angel? No,
>   spurious
> They probably heard Mary's screams and got curious.
> Then there's that star — but that's Matthew, not Luke
> And was likely just some astrological fluke
> This is not going well. Commentary all ruins it.

Christmas Stalkings

The Great Geisel

Sorry your dad's such a skeptical humanist.
Plus I'm not sure how this helps with my mission
To put you, my son, in a gen'rous condition
I'm mostly just wasting my own energy
Since the folks in the story were not refugees...
Or wait. What happened next? From the manger to
      Egypt
They fled, to escape from a child-killing regent
So that's it! That's the link. That's the single criterion
That Jesus and Mary and Joseph were *Syrian*
So, that's what we do: offer stars to the starless
Hope to the hopeless, light out of darkness
For the spirit of Christmas means helping the ones
Who don't even have mangers to bring out their sons.

Here, I paused, my breath held, waiting to see if a four-year-old's reaction was anywhere near the outburst of generosity I'd hoped for. I wanted it to be his choice — to hear him declare that he'd forego Christmas, as if he had invented altruism on the spot. And I wanted to be able to say, "Suck it, Seuss, I didn't need your help."

When at last he spoke, the boy's response was not exactly as I'd hoped. "Which one was Jesus?"

"Oh. Uh, right. He was the son. The baby."

"What did he say?"

"Uh, well...he was a baby. So he probably said, 'Wah.'"

"And then what happened?"

"Then, he grew up and said some inscrutable, but generally nice things. And then he died."

"Do you think he wiked supuh hewoes?"

"I...don't think that made it to the Gospels."

"Who do you think was his favowite supuh hewo?"

This did not mark the end of his line of questioning — the questions never end, really — but I'll spare you the rest, because this was when I figured out what mattered. I'd been looking for the story — be it a ghost story, or a Holy Ghost story — that would form some connection with my four-year-old — and, by extension, *everyone*, since we're all pretty much just four-year-olds inside. And here I was, crafting a fable in the name of peace and goodwill to all humans...when all the four-year-old wanted to know was, who was that baby? What was *he* like? Does he like the same things as me?

I didn't learn my lesson from Dr. Geisel, or from the authors of the Gospels. I almost learned it from Sir Terry Pratchett, but I got the spelling wrong: Once upon a time, a *son* came up. Or a daughter, take your pick. Every son or daughter is a story. Change the story, change the world.

Merry Christmas.

Author Notes

More than its predecessors, this story draws heavily from current events, so a bit of context might be helpful. The Syrian Refugee Crisis began in 2011, when the nation's civil war erupted, inspired in part by the Arab Spring uprisings throughout Africa and the Middle East, but exacerbated by racism and fundamentalism. Climate change also played a major role, in the form of a devastating drought that provoked widespread migration, urbanization, and unemployment. By 2015 (when I wrote my story), more than four million Syrians had fled the country — the largest exodus since World War II, perhaps the largest in human history.

The Great Geisel

In November 2015, Canada's newly-elected Liberal government announced a large-scale refugee resettlement plan. Ambitious and controversial, the plan relied upon ordinary Canadians to step up and help their new neighbours. The ethical dilemma faced by this story's narrator is a hyperbolized version of many a Canadian's quintessential Christmas quandary that year: what price philanthropy?

As of August 2016, nearly 30,000 Syrian refugees have been given new homes in Canada. To find out how to volunteer or donate, visit: http://www.cic.gc.ca/english/refugees.

Todd Pettigrew

Hark the Harried Angels Sing

I had been anticipating a Christmas that would finally be a time of peace on that little part of the Earth that fate has destined for me. I have moved since last Christmas, you see, and part of me was hoping that I had left behind the spirits that have haunted me in recent years just as surely as I had left my old bicycle in my former basement.

But it was not to be. My new abode on the North Side is even more haunted than my last. This past spring, came the spectre of a cat lady who had lived in our home long before, and who returned one rainy night. And then came back the very next day (we thought she was a goner but…). The worst part is that she didn't say "boo" or anything ghostly; she just went around the house going "*psss psss psss.*"

Then there was the angry hamadryad who came out of a tree this summer to curse my girlfriend and me for carving our names into its bark. This sappy spirit was so maddening, it nearly deprived me of my resin.

And these awful events pale next to the autumnal story I was planning on telling you: the harrowing account of *The Creaking Leeches of Leitches Creek.*

But last night came a visitation more astonishing than any of these.

It was late. So late that I was left alone as my son had long been abed, and my beloved — who has what we academics call a real job — was also sawing logs. The house was quiet, then, but my mind was not. I smelled vaguely of soot and smoke from repeated efforts to get the fire to burn properly and thus fend off the frightful oil bills that Cape Bretoners

Todd Pettigrew

know too well. I was also fretting over my Christmas gift list, for the engagement ring I had ordered had still not arrived, and my mother had just texted to let me know that she was sending money to buy my little boy a present. This was nice of her, and would be nice for him, but not so nice for me as it meant another trip to the mall. The cheque, I worried, would not cover half the cost of a remote control helicopter. And, as always, the cats were prowling, mewing, tearing the gift wrap off the presents under the tree, smashing ornaments, and wondering why I wasn't more concerned with their feeding.

I was just finishing my nightly ritual of tending to the needs of those feline fiends when, from outside, came a sound. A sound, that more than any other, simply means Christmas. Carolling.

Angels we have heard on high
Sweetly singing o'er the plains
And the mountains in reply
Echoing their joyous strains!

Such a wonder it was to hear old-fashioned carollers that I did not think at first how odd it should be that they were about so late in the evening. Nor that they were risking their lives by doing so on busy Keltic Drive. I did take note that the harmonies of the singers seemed somehow incomplete.

I did not have time to ponder any of this, for before I knew it, the carollers outside came inside. Spirits of the nether regions, I knew immediately, for they did not bother to knock or even use the door, but blew in through the closed front windows like a bitter wind off Sydney Harbour. Whereupon they finished their song.

In excelis Deeeee – ooo!

They waited for me to applaud. Artists of the next world —like the artists of this one—are constantly in need of validation. I obliged with vigorous clapping.

Christmas Stalkings

Hark the Harried Angels Sing

Once I finished my ovation, I wasn't quite sure what to say and none of the spectral singers piped up. The awkward silence gave me a chance to take a closer look at this potentially diabolical choir.

There were six of them altogether, two of whom had once been men in life and four females. Like all the spirits I've encountered, they were wispy in their outlines and nearly transparent. I could see no consistency in their apparel, either in temporal or geographic origin, which led me to believe that they had been thrown together after death, perhaps long after in some cases.

Finally, one of the carollers, a tall dark-haired woman with an aristocratic bearing, and an English accent, spoke. "Did you enjoy our song?"

"Oh, very much," I replied.

"You didn't think it sounded a little *incomplete*," she prodded, as though she had read my earlier thoughts.

"Not at all," I lied, for my general approach is not to anger ghosts. So far no spectre has ever worked any dark magic upon me, turning me into an ape, or stealing my eyeballs or whatnot, but I imagined there might always be a first time, and why provoke protoplasm?

"Well, you should have found it so," she continued, turning to stroll about the room. "Anyone who isn't entirely tone deaf could hear that we are missing an entire section."

"De tenor section," added one of the male ghosts in a low voice. And I should have known right there that this night was going to get stranger before it got normaller.

"Oh don't annoy ze poor man," said yet another ghost, a lithe female spirit with sharply hewn facial features. "If vee are to ask for his help, we want him on our side, don't vee?"

"On your side?" I said. "For what?"

"Vee need your help, darlingk," said the lithe one.

Todd Pettigrew

Now, I don't know about you, but I have always found it a little strange that these ghosts always need the help of me and a lot of people I know. They are the ones who travel through time, and walk through walls and do all manner of sorcery, and yet somehow there is always some crucial detail that only an ordinary mortal can resolve.

Well, I don't make the rules.

"Of course," I said, "I will do whatever I can to help you — do whatever it is you need. Move on? Is that it?"

"Da," said the lithe one, who I was pretty sure was Russian. "Dat is exactly vat vee need! I told you he vaz clever. He'll be ze perfect addition."

"He's too fat for a tenor," retorted the English woman. "He's a baritone by the look of him."

"A baritone vill do in a pinch, Mary," said the lithe Russian. "As you English say, beggars can't be floozies."

"Wait," I said. "Do you need me to sing a song with you? Because I happen to belong to an *a cappella* group and I do know a few tenor lines. Do you want to do *Angels we have Heard on High* again?"

"We've already done it," said the other male spirit, in an Irish brogue. "And we never sing the same one twice."

"But vee must sing zem, darlingk. And you must help us."

"Sure," I said, for I am not one of those people who is embarrassed to sing in public. Quite the reverse. I'm the one who embarrasses other people with his public singing. "But we can't be too loud," I cautioned. "My family is asleep upstairs."

"Not a problem," said the Irishman. "We're not singing here."

"What? Where are we going?"

"Vee are ze spirits of ze vurld's zingers," said Gruff Bass. "Vee zing all around ze world in the ze hope zat vone day vee join ze heavenly choir."

"Oh, I see," I replied. "Is that what happened to your other tenors? They got promoted?"

"Pablo did," came a Gaelic-tinged reply. "Nils was not so fortunate."

And an eerie quiet fell over the room, as all ghosts looked away and seemed deeply uncomfortable.

"What happened to Nils?" I demanded, entirely horror-stricken. After all, these were the wandering souls of the dead on a dark winter night. If what happened to Nils made them uneasy, it must have been soul-shattering.

Finally Mary, the Englishwoman spoke. "He was, as you mortals would say, *reincarnated*."

And all the ghosts shuddered at the word.

"Oh," I said, "that doesn't sound so bad."

"Not so bad," said the Irish ghost. "How can you, of all people, say that? Do you like being a creature of flesh and bone?"

I felt a little affronted. "It's okay."

Todd Pettigrew

"Okay!" he cried. "To be wracked by the cold winter winds? Burned by the summer sun? Subject to a hundred different diseases and then finally die a long, cold death, begging to be delivered from your misery?"

"Well, when you put it like that, I admit, it doesn't—"

"Enough of zis bickering," the Russian interrupted. "Vee must be on our vay before midnight. Tonight is ze feast of Saint Cecila, patron saint of musicians. It is our best chance to make our way to ze heavenly choir."

Before I could raise any further objections, she lifted her arms, and the whole chamber was swept up in a vortex of light and sound, as though my dining room had turned into a glowing golden bell that spun and spun, until we all reappeared...I did not know where.

We stood before a massive stone edifice, lit up by soft flood lights. A huge green dome sat in the centre with two smaller domes of the same hue, one on each side.

"Ze Berlin Cathedral," cried Gruff Bass with pride. He must have been German. *O Tannebaum*, he announced, and I realized with no small amount of anxiety that he expected me to sing the song with them right that moment. No rehearsal or anything!

"I don't know it!" I called out, which was mostly true. *O Christmas Tree*, as we English speakers call it, was a loose translation of that German original, so I did know the melody, but I certainly did not know the German words, let alone the tenor part to whatever arrangement they were singing.

"Do not worry," said one of the women who had not yet spoken, in soft French tones. "You will."

And to my delighted astonishment, I did. And I sang!
O Tannenbaum, o Tannenbaum,
wie true sind deine Blätter!
Du grünst nicht nur

Hark the Harried Angels Sing

zur Sommerzeit,
Nein auch im Winter, wenn es schneit.
O Tannenbaum, o Tannenbaum,
wie treu sind deine Blätter!

We sounded quite good, if it is not too boastful to say. As I mentioned, I have some experience singing, and the ghosts were extremely well rehearsed after Lord knows how many decades or centuries they had been at it. So while it was a shock, I have to admit, to have been transported half way around the world and asked to harmonize in the Fatherland, it was also quite a thrill.

Still, after our rendition, complete with me holding down the tenor section, there was no indication that the powers-that-be were promoting anyone to the Great Glee Club in the sky.

We moved on.

To a frozen, yet smoking, mountaintop that turned out to be a volcano in Iceland.

There I was expected to sing a song called *Snaefinner Snojkarl*, which sounded daunting until I realized it was nothing more, nor less than *Frosty the Snowman* translated into Icelandic.

En galdrar voru geymdir
í gömlu skónum hanns:
Er fékk hann þá á fætur sér
fór hann óðara í dans.
Já, Snæfinnur snjókarl,
hann var snar að lifna við,
og í leik sér brá
æði léttur þá,
– uns hann leit í sólskinið.

"Does it matter that no one can hear us?" I wondered aloud when we had finished the last chorus.

"Ze Gods can hear us," said the Russian, whose name turned out to be Natasha. Then with sudden rage, she shouted at the top of her lungs. "I know you can hear us! Vy don't you release us, you bastards!" Then she became silent and grabbed reflexively at her midsection, which, in the admittedly dim light of a nearby lava flow, looked suddenly as if it had become more opaque and solid.

"No!" she cried. "Not again." She was lifted by an unseen hand, writhing in the pain of a rapid re-embodiment, shrinking and aging backward. In seconds she was a young girl, then a baby, and even as she regained a tiny mortal form, she had disappeared.

"So," I said, "back to the land of living?"

"Zere is no time to mourn her birth," said the German bass. "Vee must move on before it is too late. If we lose an entire part again, all hope is gone. And recruiting a mortal vas a risk already. Vee cannot do it again!"

Next was Belgium, where we didn't exactly sing a song I knew, but having grown up in Canada, I was not entirely ignorant of French—thankfully it was not in Flemish—and I managed quite well:

Il est né le divin enfant,
Jouez hautbois, résonnez musette.
Il est né le divin enfant,
Chantons tous son avènement.

Sadly, my luck ran out when we reached Spain. Would it have killed them to do *Feliz Navidad*? No, it would not have killed them, because I knew for a fact that they were already dead. But no, instead of *Feliz Navidad*, we sang *El Burrito Sabanero* which, sadly, does not turn out to mean *the burrito with salsa*. More like, *my little donkey on the plains* or something like that. I think it was about riding a burro into Bethlehem. But don't quote me on that; for the night was long and *mucho loco*.

Hark the Harried Angels Sing

It was actually a catchy little tune. And whatever wondrous spell had allowed me to hold my own musically so far continued to hold me in good stead, though a saving grace was that the tenor part was only in half the song.

The women sang the verse
Con mi burrito sabanero
voy camino de Belén
Con mi burrito sabanero
voy camino de Belén
And then the men joined in on the chorus.
Si me ven, si me ven
voy camino de Belén
Si me ven, si me ven
voy camino de Belén
So Spain was a triumph, if I do say so myself. Though I still don't know the Spanish words for *burrito* or *salsa*.

And thus it went. I must admit to a certain *schadenfreude* when we lost Klaus the Gruff German Bass to reincarnation during our rendition of *Es ist für uns eine Zeit angekommen* in Lucerne, but I was saddened when the same fate befell Marie, the soft-spoken French alto, as we sang the Latvian carol, *Zie mass vētku zvani*.

Still, Mary, Patrick, Isabella and I, all now great friends on a real-name basis, sang our hearts and souls out until the dawn finally emerged over the Estonian countryside. As everyone knows, ghosts must depart this world at dawn and luckily for me, I was not stranded outside Parnu. Instead, like a warm wave, the sunlight picked me up, danced me about, and in just a few moments, deposited me back in my dining room in Leitches Creek.

It was still the night before.

Scarcely ten minutes had passed since I had first heard the ghostly chorus, and yet an epic sore throat told me it had been no dream. Spirits exist in a time outside our own.

≥ *Christmas Stalkings* ≤

Todd Pettigrew

I sat down and wondered intensely what had become of my companions. Were they fated to sing again as spirits year after year, in an endless audition for the mysterious conductors of the universe? Or had they all been doomed to walk the earth in mortal life as, indeed, I myself was?

And yet as I sat there, with the fire burning brightly in the stove, our own Tannenbaum adding its energy-efficient LED twinkling, the cats curled up on the softer presents, and my darling bride-to-be slumbering peacefully on the floor above, I recalled that this mortal life is not at all as bad as the ghosts made it out to be. It's not just sweltering days and nagging colds. It is autumn afternoons, and a sun rising on misty water. It is a quiet cigar enjoyed on a still evening, and the first buds of the spring maple. And yes, even with its obligations and debts, it is Christmas, too. We who sing the songs of this world hit plenty of wrong notes to be sure; too many, I admit. But there is enough harmony to sustain us, if we are patient enough to hear it, and courageous enough to give it voice.

And just as those thoughts had warmed my heart, I detected, far off, farther off than any earthly measure could gauge, the sound of singing. A familiar English carol, which I appreciated. There were a whole host of singers this time; none of this world, but I could still pick out a few voices that were now familiar. Mary, and Patrick, and Isabella. They had made it, after all. Perhaps this was their way of saying thank you.

As I made my way up the stairs to end the momentous night, I smiled happily. "There must be music in spite of everything," a poet once said, and I quietly joined in, somehow knowing how to sing the original eighteenth century lyrics:

God rest you merry, gentlemen,
Let nothing you dismay,

⚜ *Christmas Stalkings* ⚜

Hark the Harried Angels Sing

Remember Christ our Saviour
Was born on Christmas-day
To save poor souls from Satan's power,
Which long time had gone astray.
And it is tidings of comfort and joy.

Author Notes

One of my passions is singing, so I was eager to write a story that involved vocal music. And since this series was Christmas related, the idea of ghostly carollers seemed natural. I had to rather hastily learn several songs and familiarize myself with several different languages, but it made the story especially fun to read aloud. The nationalities of the ghosts are largely based on which accents I thought I would enjoy doing.

This tale also marked something of a new chapter in my own life, for the years between these stories contained more than their share of unrecorded dismay for the present author. I am glad to say that the dismay has now largely given way to comfort and joy.

Ken Chisholm

The Ghost of the McConnell

It was Christmas Eve, midnight, and I was standing outside the McConnell Library feeling like an idiot.

I was certain I was the victim of a practical joke, but my own natural credulity had seized hold of me. So here I was, standing by the front door of the library expecting someone — I did not know who for sure — to admit me to the library for what had been promised me to be a genuine Christmas ghost experience.

At least that was what had been promised me by the gilt-edged invitation left in my mailbox earlier that day. Jet black letters on creamy, expensive paper stock — an elaborate joke if it was a joke. But I have a circle of friends with imaginative ideas on what constitutes a holiday lark; some of them with personal links to the Regional Library administration. So I thought, as I studied the invitation: *What the hey?*

I had only a stack of DVDs to keep me indoors this evening and this ghostly invite promised to yield some sort of story that I could retail in my final months as the Cape Breton Regional Library's Storyteller in Residence.

I heard the distant peal of bells as the few fellow Sydneyites still up made their way to church services. Down the hill from the library, I saw a lonely mini-van as it sped along George Street. Beyond that, Tim Horton's and the Casino had dimmed their lights and shuttered their doors out of respect for the sanctity of the season and in compliance with provincial labour laws concerning statutory holidays.

I considered the possibility that I had made a mistake in coming and should leave, when a shadowed figure appeared behind the double set of glass doors of the library entrance, causing me nearly to jump out of my chilled skin. The figure did not seem familiar and did not make a point to greet me in any sort of friendly manner as it opened the inside set of doors. It may have been the cold wind rushing from the harbour up Falmouth Street, but I felt an ominous ice-cold shiver envelop my entire body.

The light from a street lamp fell across the person's features as he — it was definitely a man — worked the lock of the exterior doors. I took a shocked step back when he opened the door to admit me.

"You're here right on the dot," he said in a plummy, educated accent. "Good for you."

He gestured that I should enter. Dumbly, I shuffled into the foyer. In the ambient light of the night-quiet library, I confirmed my initial impression of who had invited me to this unprecedented midnight rendezvous at the McConnell. It was Charles, Prince of Wales, heir to the Throne of Canada.

"You're Prince Charles!" I postulated.

"Oh, yes, how rude. I'm Charles. You're Kevin — "

"Ken," I stammered. "I'm Ken."

"Of course, Ken," he said as he gave my hand a firm but quick grasp. "Thank you, Ken, for your wonderful volunteer service on our little charity event. Follow me."

"Charity event?" I asked.

"Yes, we are doing a paraphysical entity relocation."

"Pardon?"

"A ghost transplant," he said, as we rounded the circulation desk, past the rack of new arrivals, and towards the Nova Scotia Room where the books of Cape Breton and Maritime history are shelved. "We simply have too many spooks, and you, having almost no history to speak of, comparatively of course, don't have nearly enough."

The Ghost of the McConnell

"Actually," I interjected, "in the North End, especially around St. Patrick's Museum—"

The Royal Presence took no notice of my words.

"So to maintain the connection between our colonial citizens and the Monarchy, for the past three or four decades, we have gifted public libraries all over our dominions with our superfluous spirits."

"You mean the Commonwealth?"

"Quite."

"But libraries—?"

"They're spooky to begin with—all those people's stories contained in inky bonds on shelf after shelf." He gestured around the main section. "Besides, that's where we have the highest concentration of electroplasmic phenomena at our own various family digs."

"Why so many ghosts in palace libraries?"

"It's where we keep the gin," he said, as if that explained everything. He led me to the Nova Scotia Room.

Thanks to a paperback I had recently purchased from the McConnell sale cart for a quarter, I knew all of what he said was perfectly plausible. *The Prince and The Paranormal* detailed our current Royal Family's long association with the supernatural. Not only were almost all of the Royal residences riddled with revenants—the usual disgraced earls, wronged servant girls, decapitated relations—but also the various generations of female royal consorts all seemed to have their own pet psychic medium who would convey messages from the Other World Beyond our Corporeal Existence.

Prince Charles himself was a documented advocate of psychic healing and other such activities.

But while I had some previous confirming knowledge of all this, here I was in the darkened, empty McConnell in the middle of the night on Christmas Eve with the Prince of

Wales about to unleash some shrieking phantasm all in the name of Royal Charity. Events were moving deliriously fast, too fast for me.

"Your file says you have had some experience with ghosts?" he asked as he brought us to a table in the reference room.

"Yes." I answered, not even considering the fact that I had a file somewhere in Britain. "Last year, I was haunted by an evil ghost version of James Joyce. It's quite a tale."

"I'm sure it is. Maybe we'll have time for it after we finish our mission," he said, indicating a black knapsack sitting on the table. "Some of the boffins worked up an electromagnetic thingy that funnels the subject spirit into a receptacle for transport."

He pulled a cylindrical object from the knapsack. It was made of clear glass, so I could see the swirling mass of viscous green smoke-like substance inside.

"Is that a…gin bottle?"

"Quite. Another bit of Royal recycling, what?" the Prince said with an impish grin. "Give us a moment while I prepare to release it."

"Are these yours?" I asked, pointing to a stack of books next to his knapsack.

"They were here when we arrived," he said, busy with what looked like an old flip-phone.

"They must be donations for the Library." Being a compulsive bibliophile, I picked one of the tomes to examine. "Hmm. They're really old. And they're in Gaelic."

A folded paper tucked between the pages caught my attention, but before I could read it, the Prince said we would begin his "procedure," so I slid it into my jacket pocket. I hope you're paying attention, as this is an important plot point.

The Ghost of the McConnell

Bringing my attention back to our mission, I finally asked the question I should have asked at the outset.

"Why do you need me here?"

"You have had experience with paranormal activity, you're also familiar with the local geography and history, psychic and whatnot, and as the Library's Storyteller thingy, you are needed to sign the receipt when the Library takes legal possession, in perpetuity, of the ghost."

"Don't you mean when the ghost takes possession of the Library?"

"Quite," he said, as he placed the bottle filled with the paranormally potent presence on the tiled floor.

I was more than a little worried to see the bottle rock and sway and make abrupt violent hops on its own power. "It looks...angry," I said.

"They're all like that. The boffins have a way of dampening the psychic energy." He waved the flip phone. "That takes some of the bite out of them. Now when I give the signal say, 'Spirit come forth'..."

"Spirit, come forth?" I repeated.

"Not now!"

But it was too late.

The bottle exploded, showering both of us with sharp shards of glass and giving the freed ghost an opportunity to materialize with all of its force intact.

The room was filled with a harrowing sound. It came like the wind through the silence of the night, a long, deep mutter, then a rising howl, and then the sad moan in which it died away. Again and again it sounded, the whole air throbbing with it, strident, wild and menacing. Together we looked up at the source of this unearthly sound to be confronted with the sight of an enormous spectral dog towering over us by a least half a meter. A hound it was, an enormous green glowing hound, but not such a hound as mortal eyes have ever seen.

Its eyes gleamed with a malicious green intensity; its needle sharp, oversized fangs slobbered with green dripping slime, its shaggy green paws looked more like a raptor's razor talons. And atop is massive green head was the most incongruent sight of all: a large flouncy bow that, if not for its green tinge, I would have sworn was a cloying pink.

"It's a giant collie," I said, in a whisper.

"If I know my breeds, and I do, it's a giant miniature collie," the Prince replied.

The beast growled and bared its fangs even more.

"Then why is it so huge?"

"It's the nature of little dogs to come back as ghost dogs the size they thought they were in life. I once encountered a ghost Chihuahua the size of an African bull elephant —"

The dog fixed its angry green eyes on us.

"I think this one still has all of its bite," I said. "Do you think we can outrun it?" I turned to the Prince only to find empty air and the sound of his fleeing footfalls heading toward the front door.

"Good doggy?" I ventured.

The ghost dog would have none of it and went back on its haunches, readying itself to leap at my terrified self.

 I ran.

A clatter of ghostly paws told me I had a pursuer. Rounding the reference desk, my foot caught on one of the plastic shopping baskets available to library patrons to carry their selections to the circulation desk. I sprawled across the floor, shutting my eyes to my imminent demise.

A thud told me the beast's paws had landed astride my supine form. Something wet, but so cold it burned, dripped on my cheek. Something like the Cold Breath of the Grave defiled the hairs on my head.

Christmas Stalkings

The Ghost of the McConnell

This was it.

"Bobby, no," a quiet voice said.

The presence above me hesitated.

"Bobby, come here," the voice said, quiet and firm.

A small snarl of confusion sounded above me. I felt the presence move quietly from me and pad toward the small, calm voice.

I opened my eyes.

There, in the center of the library, stood the ghostly form of a young woman, lithe of body, with gentle yet wise eyes, dressed in a long dress of homespun. She looked perfectly natural except for the benign, pale blue aura radiating from her form.

The monstrous ghostly canine lay at her feet, its head between its paws, its big fierce eyes now more collie-like and gazing up at her with doggy adoration.

"Good Bobby," the young woman said. "And let's take that silly thing from you."

She extended her arm and pulled the flouncy ribbon from the beast's massive skull. As it fell away, it dissolved into a cloud of green pinpricks of light, and the ghost dog's huge tail swung back and forth in joy, threatening to sweep away books, chairs, and table. But before the damage could be done, the form of the dog shrunk until it was the regular size of a miniature collie.

"Bit of a runt, isn't it?" the Prince said, now beside me. Where he had hidden himself while I was in peril from the hell hound I never learned.

"You found me after all this time," the woman said, as the small dog leapt happily into her arms. They now shared the same blue hue. "Aren't you a smart boy?"

"Who do you think she is?" the Prince asked.

Ken Chisholm

Christmas Stalkings

The Ghost of the McConnell

"I'm not sure, but I know she's a Gillis," I said. "And if I know my Gillises, and I do, she's a Grand Mira Gillis."

"Honestly?"

"Who's the local guide here?"

"Quite."

Besides their familial physical resemblances, the Grand Mira Gillae was one of the founding Gaelic communities on the island and had a well-known history of association with the supernatural. Family history held the appearance of "Faerie Lights" along the Mira River, where the clan settled after coming to Cape Breton from Scotland, infallibly foretold death and tragedy to their small community.

Then I noticed the piece of paper at the ghost woman's feet. It was the paper I had removed from the donated Gaelic book—which I am sure you all remember as that important plot point earlier.

I approached the woman and dog, who were busy enjoying their reunion, and picked it up. It was printed with several stanzas of Gaelic verse. I handed it to her.

"Look Bobby, it's my poem about you and how much I missed you when my father sold you to that passing Royal Kennel Master just before we left for the New World," she said, showing the paper to the dog, who studied it as if he could read the printed words. "Father felt so bad that he had copies of my poem printed in Sydney to cheer me up."

"It's a ghost," I whispered.

"Of course, it's a ghost," The Prince said. "It's two of them, in fact."

"No, the poem is a ghost," I said to the Prince's uncomprehending face. "A ghost is a printed item of which no copies are known to exist. That poem is probably one of the first Gaelic works ever printed on Cape Breton Island."

"Then I need to take it to the British Museum," the Prince said, reaching for the paper in the young woman's hand.

Christmas Stalkings

Bobby growled and snapped at his fingers.

"If you take that paper," I said, "you'll have to take the dog as well."

"I'll not be parted from my Bobby," the woman said, hugging both him and the paper more tightly to her body. "Not after we found each other again."

The Prince withdrew his hand, reluctantly.

"Quite."

"Thank you, sir," she said to me. "Bobby was the only thing I missed from back home. Now I am happy."

"Actually, I'm the one—" the Prince began.

"It's time for us to be going, isn't it?" I said.

The Prince nodded in resigned agreement.

"Come back and visit," the woman said, more to me than the Prince. She turned and took in the library around her and exclaimed, "Look Bobby, books! We shall have to read them all!"

The Prince and I made our way out of the front entrance, leaving the young woman and Bobby to get re-acquainted.

On the sidewalk, the Prince spoke into his flip phone. "Mission accomplished. Ready for retrieval."

While we waited, I asked him how he chose the McConnell for this particular spirit.

"Oh, the usual: once we contain the ghost thingy, we have a séance. Ouija board, you know, and then we *Goggle* the exact location. The doggy must have been directing us here all the time."

"There you go."

"So, two ghosts for the price of one," he said, quite pleased with himself. "Just proves the Monarchy is still an effective and relevant institution, right?"

Before I could disagree, a black nylon rope with a clip attached dropped from the sky. The Prince attached it to his belt and before I could speak, he was swiftly pulled upwards to a black, silently-hovering helicopter.

And then he was gone.

I walked up the ramp to the library's front entrance so I could look into the window. The young woman knelt on the floor in front of the magazine rack, reading aloud to Bobby. He sat in front of her, tilted head following her every syllable. She looked up, saw me and smiled.

I waved a good-bye and walked back down the ramp heading for home. Christmas morning was dawning fast in the eastern sky over the spires of St. Theresa's Church. I looked forward to a day of cheer among the oblivious living.

I still felt like an idiot, but at least, for this Christmas, I'd been a useful idiot.

Author Notes

This story, with the Prince of Wales as my antagonist, was meant for the year after "Joyce to the World," but a serious illness forced me to bow out. However, I completed it for the next one which turned out to be the final year of this particular iteration of Gaudy Night.

My inspiration was *The Prince and The Paranormal*, a book I found on the twenty-five cent cart of paperbacks of library discards to be found in the McConnell's lobby. Some of the lore of haunted palaces comes from that book as well as the "history" of Charles' involvement with the paranormal and other esoteric and metaphysical beliefs. My plan was always

Ken Chisholm

to have a more wistful ending and a few odds and ends I picked up along the way — a part of a book on publishing about "ghosts" (actually referring to a juvenile poem by James Joyce his father had printed!) gave me one element, an evening of storytelling collection in Grand Mira sponsored by the Regional Library and the Beaton Institute introduced me to the Gaelic folk beliefs of the Gillis families there, and a description of the ghost dog was literally cut and pasted from an online version of Conan Doyle's *The Hound of The Baskervilles* — filled out the tale. I even got to mention the shopping baskets available for library patrons that undoubtedly only a few of them know are there for their convenience.

For both stories in this anthology, my main object was to have fun writing them with the hope the audience would have fun listening to them (and I was very conscious they would be heard rather than read). To do that, I cut any exposition and description of person and place to the bare minimum and tried to make up for lapses in logic and plausibility by using storytelling drive and humour. Preparing these stories for publication, with the direction of our perceptive editors, I decided not to put back in the bits I left out and hope that the *High Spirits* with which they were written would entertain my audience of readers.

The Authors

Ken Chisholm

Ken Chisholm lives in Sydney, Nova Scotia, where he writes a newspaper column for the Cape Breton Post, has held the post of Storyteller In Residence for the Cape Breton Regional Library, writes songs, writes plays, and writes fiction, but never poetry. He also performs onstage as an actor, singer, and musician, but can't dance (so don't ask him).

Todd Pettigrew

Originally from New Hamburg, Ontario, Todd Pettigrew studied English and Theatre at the University of Western Ontario, McMaster University and the University of Waterloo, where he earned his Ph.D. in 1998.

After a brief stint in publishing, he came to Cape Breton to take up a faculty position at Cape Breton University (then the University College of Cape Breton) in 2000. He is now Associate Professor of English in the Department of Cultural and Creative Studies, and is the author of numerous scholarly publications, including an award-winning monograph, "Shakespeare and the Practice of Physic" (2007).

For many years he has been active in local theatre, but now directs most of his creative energy towards music and writing fiction. He lives in Leitches Creek with his wife, two sons, and more cats than many think is advisable.

Scott Sharplin

Scott Sharplin grew up in Edmonton, Alberta, where a lively theatre scene and a procession of inspiring English teachers conspired to make a playwright out of him. After earning his B.A. (Honours) at the University of Alberta, he moved to Montreal to study playwriting at the National Theatre School of Canada, but an ill-timed ice storm sent him packing. Since then, he has been Artistic Director of two theatre companies, managed three video stores (remember *those?*), earned an M.A. in Humanities Computing, and worked for three post-secondary institutions.

Scott's previously published work includes the scripts "Burnt Remains" (in *Staging Alternative Albertas,* Playwrights Canada Press, 2002), "Purity Test" (in *Three on the Boards,* Signature Editions, 2008), and "The Trial of Salomé" (in *Hot Thespian Action,* Athabasca University Press, 2008). His plays have been produced across Canada, and he is a member of the Playwrights Guild of Canada and the Playwrights Atlantic Resource Centre. In addition to playwriting, Scott writes role-playing games, journalistic non-fiction, short stories, and beer-themed haiku. His other freelance artistic work includes acting, dramaturgy, and arts administration.

In 2009, Scott moved to Sydney with his wife, Dr. Sheila Christie, to teach at Cape Breton University. Two years later, they had a son, whose presence looms large in all Scott's subsequent writing.

You can follow Scott online by bookmarking his blog, http://mapledanish.com, or subscribing to his messy missives at http://www.tinyletter.com/scottsharplin.

Jenn Tubrett

Jenn Tubrett is a writer from Sydney. Nova Scotia. Her roots are in Theatre. She grew to love the English language as an actor and quickly moved into playwrighting. In 2010, during the 39th Elizabeth Boardmore One Act Play Festival at the Boardmore Theatre in Sydney, Nova Scotia, Tubrett took home the award for Best Original Script with her romp comedy *Notte Del Partito*.

Shortly after that she began meeting with a group of local writers and continues to do so to this day. They call themselves The Dead Puppets Society. It is with this group and through creating a series of horror-themed Halloween shows (The *Tales from the Bottom of the Well* series, the *Black Jack* series, and participating as an actor in *Frankenstein*) that she discovered the joy of writing horror. It is also through this group that she gained the confidence and guidance to write narrative.

Tubrett has published twice before with Third Person Press; first in 2012 with her Sci-Fi/Horror short story "Our Last Vacation" as part of *Unearthed*, Volume 3 of the Speculative Elements Series and in 2014, with her dystopian short story "Epilogue" as a part of *Flashpoint,* Volume 4 in the Speculative Elements Series. "Bucky's Ghost" marks her third publication with Third Person Press.

Gaudy Nights at the McConnell Library

In the fall of 2010, I approached Dr. Todd Pettigrew from Cape Breton University's English Department about the possibility of speaking at the McConnell Memorial Library in Sydney, Nova Scotia about some of the Canadian authors that our New Horizon's Seniors' Book Clubs were reading. Being a Robertson Davies devotee and scholar, Todd suggested he could speak about him, as he wrote many of his novels later in life, and claimed that you can best appreciate a novel when you are close in age to the author when the book was written. At that point we had only thirty titles in our book club collection, and only one by Davies, so Todd made a wonderful suggestion!

To commemorate the 15th anniversary of Davies' death that December, he proposed that we hold an event to raise money to purchase more books for the book clubs. Todd's idea was to resurrect the "Gaudy Night" readings, Davies' tradition of telling a ghost story at the annual Massey College Christmas party at the University of Toronto. Davies did this for the eighteen years he was the Master of the College, for the amusement of those attending the celebrations. These spooky, humourous, Christmas-themed ghost stories were eventually published by Penguin Canada in 1982 in the collection "High Spirits."

For the first two years we offered this event, Todd was joined by Scott Sharplin from the CBU Drama Department to read three of Davies' ghost stories. Both Todd and Scott are acclaimed performers in the CBU and community theatre circles with the dramatic flair to do justice to these stories, so the events were great successes. In the third year, Todd contributed an original story while Scott and Cape Breton

Regional Library's Storyteller in Residence, Ken Chisholm, also an accomplished thespian, read stories by Davies. By the fourth year, all three contributed original stories, so we were truly offering our own homegrown Gaudy Night! In our sixth year, actor and author Jenn Tubrett joined the cast and has contributed her story to this collection as well.

Over the six years, hundreds of dollars in donations were collected at the Gaudy Night events to support the Library's Seniors' Book Clubs across the region. These resources allowed us to purchase over forty sets of books that kept our voracious readers happy until we were able to secure another New Horizons for Seniors' grant that allowed us to purchase over one hundred new sets of books to serve the growing demand for good reads. This let us expand our book clubs beyond those that met at library branches to those in rural areas served by our bookmobiles and to clubs meeting in the community. To date, there are thirty book clubs served by this collection, and more are taking advantage of it every year.

This has been a great success story, with audiences looking forward each year to enjoying the creativity and dramatic readings of these wonderful local thespians, and the Cape Breton Regional Library (and book club members!) appreciating the ongoing support for book clubs in our community.

Chris Thomson, Programs
Cape Breton Regional Library
Sydney, Nova Scotia
August 2016

Afterword

There is something special about stories told in the oral tradition. A freshness in the approach. An immediate intimacy that the written word can sometimes leave behind. The stories in this volume were first written down, of course, but the writers knew they would be presenting them aloud, and as a result, they each reflect the relationship with an audience they were entertaining.

In the spring of 2016, Chris Thomson of the McConnell library, approached Third Person Press about whether we'd be interested in looking at this collection. At the time we were technically open only to novel submissions, but when we heard who had authored these stories we were definitely interested in reading them. It took very little time for us to know that this was an unusually clever, cohesive, and unique set of stories—ones that celebrate not only Christmas and ghosts, but also literature, illustrious writers, libraries, history, books, humour and word play. How could we resist?

We had great fun pulling it together, and see *Christmas Stalkings* becoming a classic, not only to Cape Bretoners, but also to those who have yet to fully discover the prodigious talent that thrives on this Island.

A spirited toast to the authors for sharing their creativity with the rest of us and to the dedicated staff at the McConnell Memorial Library, Sydney, Nova Scotia, and all of the libraries in the regional district, for bringing out some of the best in Cape Breton writing. And, as they were meant to be told stories, we suggest that they—perhaps during the season of Advent—be read aloud.

Nancy, Sherry and Julie, Editors
Northside, Cape Breton
2016

Christmas Stalkings

About Third Person Press

Since its founding in 2007, Cape Breton writers, Julie A. Serroul, Sherry D. Ramsey and Nancy SM Waldman have published seven volumes of high-quality fiction by local and regional authors.

This small, independent press specializes in speculative fiction: science fiction, fantasy, horror and the other sub-genres that fall into the "unreal-fiction" category. The work—calling for, reading, evaluating, and responding to submissions; advising, editing, revising, proofreading, type-setting, illustrating, designing, formatting print and e-books; publicizing, launching and promoting the products—is accomplished part-time by these three busy women. It is definitely a labour of love.

Close to forty talented writers have had their work published by Third Person Press and many more have been given advice and encouragement for their writing. The press has now turned its attention to novels by writers from Atlantic Canada. The first one, *Rise of the Mudmen*, will be published in 2017.

Stay in touch:
website: www.thirdpersonpress.com
email: thirdpersonpress@gmail.com
Facebook: www.facebook.com/thirdpersonpress/
Twitter: @3rdpersonpress

⋆ *Christmas Stalkings* ⋆

The Books

Coming in 2017 from Third Person Press

Rise of the Mudmen
by James FW Thompson

"I'm glad you woke me up," his dad said, his features softening, but still holding onto a trace of seriousness. "I had a bad dream."

After a few seconds, Alex asked "About what?"

"I don't really know."

"Oh." That answer was somehow disappointing. Alex had almost hoped that his father had the same dream he did; if it scared his dad, then it was all right for him to be scared of it too.

"Just...," his dad continued, "bad stuff. There's...there's a lot happening, you know? In the world? Stuff falling apart."

Alex, Nicole, David, and Kaitlyn are about to have their world torn apart.

Something bad is happening, but even the adults don't seem to know what it is — or if they do, they're not saying. When that something reaches the small island of Cape Breton, it's too late to do anything but run and hide. Fourteen-year-old Alex and a group of kids thrown together by the havoc must survive a nightmare place of missing parents, a school in flames, and neighborhoods overrun by the bloodthirsty creatures they call "mudmen."

As they struggle to create a safe haven, defend themselves, and learn to take care of each other, they discover that there's more than one kind of enemy...and that sometimes the worst ones come from within.

If you liked *Stranger Things*, *Stand By Me*, and *The Goonies* you'll love this fast-paced adventure set in the 1980s. It will keep you turning pages from start to finish.

James FW Thompson is a Cape Breton playwright, writer, artist, actor, teacher, mentor, and new father.

Christmas Stalkings

www.ingramcontent.com/pod-product-compliance
Lightning Source LLC
Chambersburg PA
CBHW071956170626
46813CB00005B/1905